Queen of the Oaks

The Chronicles of

Burnam Tau'roh

Book Three

Also by Walter G. Klimczak

Falling in the Garden
This Place Only
My Forgotten Life
Blackberry Way
Halfway Down the Stairs
The Oak Hotel
The Painted Lighthouse

Praise for *Falling in the Garden*

Queen of the Oaks

The Chronicles of Burnam Tau'roh
Book Three

Walter G. Klimczak

Autumn Harbor Press

Atlanta, GA

Queen of the Oaks

The Chronicles of Burnam Tau'roh

Book Three

Autumn Harbor Press

April 2011

978-0-9825732-3-5

For more information about Autumn Harbor books,
please visit our website @ www.autumnharbor.com

This book is dedicated to
Kayleigh and Rylyn Monahan

"When the oak is felled, the whole forest echoes with its fall."

Thomas Carlyle

"Bring the past only if you are going to build from it."

Doménico Cieri Estrada

Chiromancy (n.)

The art of foretelling the future
through the study of the palm.

Contents

Pronunciation Guide

Cast of Characters

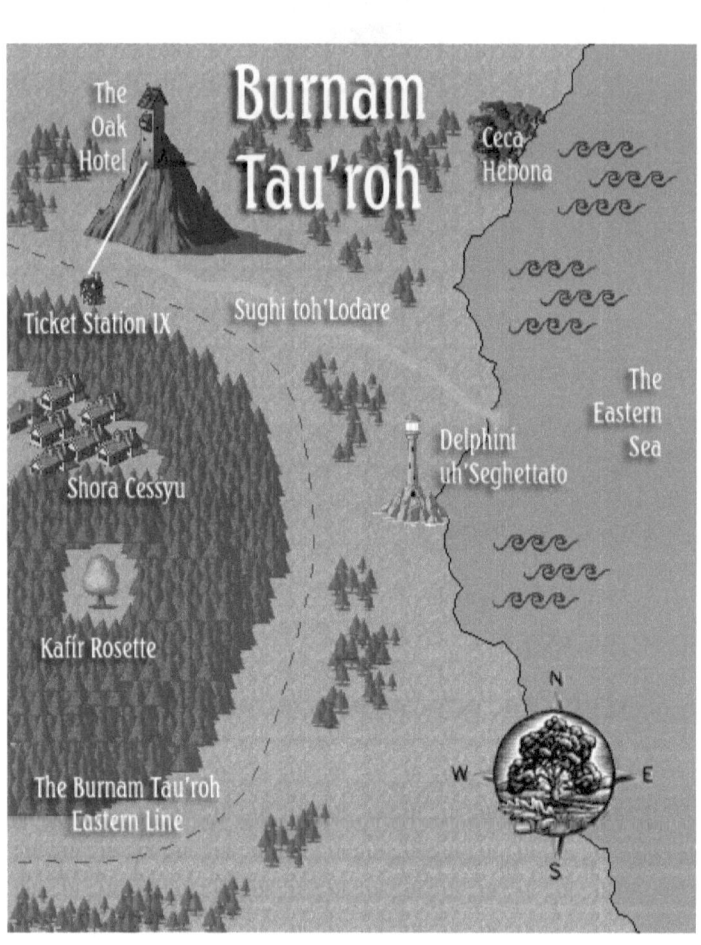

1. Trokamano Orchard

Over and over, the unceasing sound of train wheels on tracks ticked away the unbearable slip and passage of time. Kayleigh sat beside Rylyn, holding her hand while Lincoln (opposite them) impatiently watched the forest pass by in a steady, green blur.

There were other passengers in their car. An older woman dressed in purple sat near the exit door, her stubby fingers worrying over the bright, purple beads of her necklace. Two younger women sat a few seats behind them, reading from a shared book. A middle-aged man with dark hair (dressed as Sheenie Tosh had been dressed when Lincoln first met her, hooded cloak and all) sat silently in the rear. Lincoln glanced at the darkly dressed man occasionally, but the stranger's eyes were locked on some point beyond the walls of the train car.

Kayleigh had tried over and over to ask questions, but finally gave up. Each time she spoke, Rylyn grew more upset and could barely speak. The girl sat there now, eyes closed, taking slow breaths.

"How far back do you think we came?" Lincoln asked.

Kayleigh looked over at him and sighed. "I'm not sure. Didn't Creek say that one of the letters he found was over a hundred and eighty years old?"

Lincoln nodded.

"It probably doesn't matter how far back we came," Kayleigh mused, "As long as we find these three sisters."

The train bounced, then shook slightly as it turned left with the tracks.

"I don't know," Lincoln whispered, "Just being here, in this different time, makes me nervous. I was starting to get used to being in Burnam Tau'roh, but this just weirds me out."

Kayleigh glanced from the now sleeping form of Rylyn to him. "I know what you mean. So… what's the deal with Mona? If we've gone this far back in time, how could she possibly be alive?"

Lincoln just shook his head and said, impatiently, "I just wish this train would go faster. We're not going to get any answers until we see her. I've been waiting for this train to talk, too, the way BTEL #3 did. I guess that upgrade hasn't been made yet."

The train continued along the northeastern arc of the Burnam Tau'roh Eastern Line. Neither Kayleigh nor Lincoln could gauge the passage of time. When the train did stop, Rylyn stirred from her sleep, but shook her head when they stood.

"No," she said quietly. "This is Ticket Station IX. We're one more up."

The three female passengers rose from their seats and exited the train, but no new passengers boarded. The mysterious man remained. Lincoln pointed him out to Rylyn and she whispered that his name was Eliot Hughs, a reclusive artist rarely seen in public. When the train chugged back to life, Lincoln stood and stretched. When he sat back down, he was holding the book the two younger women had been reading. "They forgot their book," he murmured.

Taking the book from him, Rylyn frowned. "No, they did not *forget* it. It was left behind intentionally."

Kayleigh glanced at the title. *Evil Doth Flow From The Sea.*

"Nice title," she said, "But why did they leave it?"

Stretching, not as visibly upset as earlier, Rylyn handed the book back to Lincoln. "There are more Traders on the Eastern Sea than ever now," she explained, "A growing number of people are banding together in protest of trading. Oddly enough, a Trader has just been elected to the mayorship of Burnam Tau'roh. He's being sworn in tomorrow. Dissenters believe that all the knowledge the Traders bring in will destroy us. I can only imagine how upset they are knowing a Trader will be leading us."

"Um," Kayleigh said, "Who is the mayor now?"

Rylyn smiled. "A woman by the name of Nova Reckór, probably the best mayor we've ever had. She's already served three full terms, though, and her time is up."

"I'm afraid to ask who the new mayor is?" Lincoln said, flipping through the book.

Rylyn looked puzzled at this and turned to Kayleigh.

"Let me guess… Truman Stitch," Kayleigh said.

"That… is correct," Rylyn said.

"For crying out loud," Lincoln said, snapping the book shut. "Are we ever going to be rid that guy!"

Rylyn looked downcast and said, mostly to herself, "There is more going on here than Mona has told me."

Lincoln laughed. "We should have shirts made with those words on the front."

Kayleigh smirked at him, then allowed herself a smile. She glanced at Rylyn, who looked even more troubled.

Soon enough, the train began to slow, brakes squealing. This ticket station here was smaller and there were no people waiting to board. When the train pulled off and fled slowly around a bend into the forest, Rylyn led them across the tracks and down a wide, dirt road. There were parallel ruts in the center, presumably made by carts or carriages. Lincoln imagined the late 1800's in the American South. The further they walked, the more fragrant the air grew. The randomness of scraggly trees changed and to either side of them a phalanx of short, robust trees boasted innumerable pink, fist-sized blossoms.

Rylyn's pace picked up as they neared a tall, metal gate. Before she could even reach out to pull up the clasp, it swung open and a middle-aged man walked out to greet her. His face was grave and his actions were jerky and nervous. His eyes moved from Kayleigh and Lincoln back to Rylyn.

Rylyn took the older man's hand and spoke quickly, "Peter, tell me—"

"Mona sits in the tea room," he stuttered, "She is no worse nor better than when you left."

Peter Keage, who had for years been the head groundskeeper and in charge of over thirty skilled laborers, looked helpless. His fingers, which had been wringing themselves in a mad dance, grew limp as he dropped his arms.

"Thank you," Rylyn said to him with a wan smile, then turned to Lincoln and Kayleigh. "We must go to her now."

Through the gate and past a few more of the blossom-adorned trees, Kayleigh felt her breath catch in her chest. Lincoln actually stopped momentarily as the sight before him overwhelmed his senses.

They stood at the base of a slowly rising hill. At the top sat a beautiful, white farmhouse, as charming as a large fairy tale cottage. Surrounding this expansive structure were not hundreds, but perhaps thousands of trees. Upon each tree were small, pink orbs weighing the boughs in vast number. A cool breeze whispered down from the top of the hill and the scent that assaulted them was magnificent. Whatever this fruit was, Lincoln could hardly contain himself. Kayleigh was surprised to discover she'd taken a full five steps toward the nearest of the trees.

"Whoa!" Rylyn said, grabbing Kayleigh's arm and pulling her back. "You don't want to be doing that. Rapture figs are only edible at the end of the season and that's another two months from now."

"Do they taste bad now?" Lincoln asked.

Rylyn grimaced. "From what I hear, they taste fine no matter when they're picked, but until first frost they're poisonous. You've never eaten a rapture fig?"

A bit shaken, Kayleigh said, "We're not from around here."

Already making her way up a narrow path through the trees, Rylyn motioned them upward.

Each step closer to the white house was like walking through a horrible temptation.

"It smells so amazing," Lincoln said, more to himself, but Kayleigh agreed.

"It's too bad we didn't land two months later," she added.

They continued to climb the path in silence.

Near the top, Rylyn turned to them. Emotion again overwhelmed her face. "Mona wishes for you to see her alone. I will go along first and check on her. Wait a moment, then come up to the house."

Rylyn disappeared toward the house and they did as they were told, waiting nervously for about a minute.

Taking Kayleigh's hand, Lincoln led them up the pebbled path to a wide flight of a dozen or so wooden steps. The craftsmanship of the house was remarkable. Each board and joint had been carefully planned out and perfectly executed. The grand porch was, Kayleigh thought with a smile, wide enough to host a small banquet. Hung at evenly spaced intervals were peat-bottomed baskets that held streamers of fern-like plants.

Before them waited a stained-glass paned door.

Noticing that the straps of his backpack were coming undone, Kayleigh moved behind Lincoln and tugged until it was again secure on his back.

"I can't believe I lost my backpack when we fell into the Eastern Sea," she said, frowning.

"Don't worry about it," Lincoln said. "Luckily, we had the important stuff in mine. You mostly had food."

The closed door still waited before them.

"Um…" Lincoln said softly. "You should probably be the one to go in first."

"Chicken," Kayleigh said, smiling. She stepped forward and, without knocking, opened the door.

The interior was immaculate, every surface free of dust. Pots, pans and other various sized copper and pewter containers hung from various places. Stacked neatly just about everywhere were sparkling jars.

A large island counter stood at the rear of the room, as clean as an operating table.

"Well I'll be," a soft voice spoke. Lincoln glanced around, confused as to where it had come from. Kayleigh, however, had already crossed half the room. Lincoln followed, looking over her shoulder at the woman sitting in a wooden rocking chair before a dark fireplace.

Defying all logic and reason, it was truly Mona Tarok. Not simply some ancestor of the woman they knew from the Oak Hotel, but the very same. She did, however, appear older. They noticed at once the extra creases in her face and the delicate way her hands rested in her lap.

Kayleigh stopped before her and knelt, taking the worn hands carefully into her own.

Lincoln stood a foot behind, shaking his head lightly.

"You don't look like you're dying, Mona," he said, surprised that any sound had come from him at all.

The woman's eyes sparkled. She drew in a shaky breath, then began to speak.

"Before you ask your questions, dear ones, I wish to tell you a story. When I was a young girl of about six years old, my father took me to the harvest fair. It was the very first harvest fair in Burnam Tau'roh. Everyone gathered at the marketplace a few miles west of the orchard. It was simply splendid. My father sold his prized rapture fig jams and candies. There was singing and games and Traders brought whatever magic they had found out on the sea. But I will always remember that day because of the Corci sisters."

Lincoln's eyes widened as he sat beside Kayleigh, setting a hand gently against her back. Kayleigh did not turn, but was transfixed by the old woman's words. Mona continued, her voice amazingly strong:

"Behind all of the festivities, pitched against a young willow tree, was a tent. The fabric was faded and torn, but inside were three of the sweetest little girls you ever saw. Their mother sat behind them (they had no father) and before long there was a line of over fifty people waiting to see these girls.

"Luckily, I discovered the tent much earlier while my father was first setting up his booth. At first, I thought they were just there to see the fair. They were about seven years old, a year older than I was, and identical triplets. Well, nearly identical. Their faces were the same, but one was blonde, one brunette and the other a redhead. Curious, I stood before the tent flap and introduced myself. Their mother, a short, rather homely woman, asked me to have a seat before the girls.

"We all sat on old stools, myself included, and I knew at once that something was wrong. When they each spoke their name in greeting, their eyes were focused on something far behind me.

"'They cannot see,' their mother explained. I didn't know what to say to this, but the first girl—Mynah, with the blonde hair—reached forward and took my left hand in hers. She caressed my palm with her soft, cool fingers. She did this for a long time, tracing each line, and I felt my eyelids slowly closing. Finally, she pulled back and said in a soft voice, 'You will be the custodian of a great, wooden citadel. People will travel great distances to see you.' I looked over at their mother, who stared at me with wide, meaningful eyes. I turned slightly to the middle girl, the red-headed Hymna, and she took my hand without pause. Her touch was more insistent, though equally as gentle. She said, 'Your light shall never go out so long as your wards return with the Trokamano Pandiment.'"

"No way," Kayleigh breathed.

"Finally, the third sister took my hand. Ahnmy's touch was more gentle. Like yours, Kayleigh. She spent the least amount of time tracing my palm. When she spoke, she leaned close to me and kept my eyes with hers. She spoke each word with extreme precision. 'The year the evil one takes rein of this town, Kayleigh and Lincoln will appear where the lighthouse shall stand. They will tell you what needs to be done. Send someone to meet them on midsummer morn.

"The remainder of the day is not as clear to me. I know that when I left the tent, the town archivist, Iris Tonah, was standing right outside. She asked me what the girls had said. I told her what I remembered and she wrote it down in a thick book. I know that my father and I spent that evening at the Tompkins Apiary. Old Ben Tompkins and my Dad did business together, experimenting with rapture figs and honey to make the most amazing candies. While they sat inside and talked, I wandered around the hills. The sound of the bees in their hives calmed me. The aroma of the foxglove, which ran like a spring stream beyond the hives in purple splendor, made me sleepy. It was twilight then, and growing darker. I fell asleep right there between the foxglove and a hedge of blackberries.

"You see, children, part of me thinks I've been dreaming all these years. Maybe I just fell asleep on that hill and have only just now awoken. Oh, I know that sounds silly, but that's what it feels like. And now it is midsummer and Rylyn has brought you to me. I'm sorry for the melodrama I used to get you here so quickly, but I have been waiting for quite some time. I'm not dying. Not at this moment, at least. I wanted to make sure you came straight away."

"You look and sound so much like our Mona," Kayleigh began, cautiously, "But you can't be."

"Our Mona is younger," Lincoln said to Kayleigh, then turned to Mona. "Maybe you're aging backward."

Mona smiled at this, but shook her head. "I'm not so sure about that, young man."

"Me neither," Kayleigh said. "Let's think about those fortunes for a minute. The first one is easy, about being a custodian of a wooden palace. That's the Oak Hotel."

Mona's eyes widened. "I received a letter from our mayor elect just yesterday. He has asked that I take up the post of head matron at a trader's hostel that will be built atop Mount Aikona. He also asked that I take on the responsibility as the new archivist of Burnam Tau'roh."

"That answers that," Lincoln said. Mona leaned forward.

"So what, then, about my light never going out if my wards return with this Trokamano Pandiment. I don't even know what a Pandiment is."

"I think that we are your wards, Mona. Pandiments are a bit difficult to explain, but we actually came here to collect another Pandiment. The Pandiment of Time."

"We're supposed to meet up with the same three girls you spoke about," Lincoln said.

"But I guess they're not girls anymore," Kayleigh added. "Are they?"

Mona frowned, "I'm sorry to say that they're not. In fact, the Corci sisters passed away only a week ago."

Standing, Lincoln huffed. "Okay, that's just a bit convenient, isn't it? Stitch probably figured out we were coming and had them killed."

Mona stood, alarmed. "Truman Stitch truly is the evil one, then? You speak as if you know him."

"Oh, we know him," Kayleigh said, standing now as well. "But hold on. The Truman Stitch in our time has done some pretty horrible things, but he's never done anything bad to you, Mona. Ever. It's strange, but it's almost as if he's been protecting you and the Oak Hotel all this time."

Deep in thought, Mona moved across the room toward the kitchen area. Lincoln rose and he and Kayleigh followed her. Stopping at a large table, Mona retrieved two wooden bowls and two spoons and set them side by side.

"Lincoln," she said, a bit more calmly, "Would you be a dear and get one of the jars from the ice box over there? One with a purple lid, please."

Lincoln did as instructed.

Taking the large Mason jar from him, Mona carefully unsealed the cap and produced a long, thin ladle. With it, she spooned several dollops of the dark, rich-looking preserve into each of the two bowls. When she was done, she set the ladle in a sink, licked the tip of her index finger and smiled at them.

"Go ahead," she said, "I believe this is your first time? Rylyn said you've never heard of rapture figs."

Taking their bowls, Kayleigh and Lincoln were overwhelmed by the divine aroma. The rich preserve, filled with tender pieces of fruit, was beyond words. It was as if the purest essences of their favorite fruits had been combined. Halfway through his bowl, Lincoln looked up at Kayleigh and said, "I think I know now what makes that Cherry Ace soda taste so good."

Kayleigh nodded, savoring another spoonful of fruit.

When they finished, Mona took their bowls and spoons and led them to the far side of the kitchen where they sat upon low wooden stools.

"You have tasted one of my favorite harvests—seven years ago. Rapture figs grow all the sweeter the longer they are kept. But," she said with a wink, "You have to know how to preserve them."

They sat in comfortable silence for a while, then Mona said, "I am afraid for the two of you. You seem to be here to help me, but it appears you are in danger from this Trader, Truman Stitch."

"I think the important thing is that you do what he asks," Kayleigh sighed. "We'll try to find the Trokamano Pandiment, though I have no idea where we're going to look. Burnam Tau'roh is a lot different than what we're used to."

"You're from a time in the future, then?" Mona asked in awe, the light of a child in her eyes.

Somewhat hesitantly, Lincoln said, "Yes, but I'm not sure how much we should say."

"My guess is that anything we say has already affected what's happened, like our note," Kayleigh added. "Maybe changing things by going back in time isn't possible…"

Lincoln nodded thoughtfully, though was obviously still troubled.

Mona shook her head and smiled, which shed a bit of light through their cloudy parlay.

"You must let my orchard be your haven while you're here in *my* time," Mona said. "Whatever it is you have to do, you can always come back here and I'll do whatever I can to help."

Kayleigh stood and hugged her. "You have done that for us many times before."

Laughing, Lincoln agreed and said, "At least, you will."

Later that evening, they sat side by side on the front porch, sipping icy lemon water from tall, smoky glasses.

"We need to stay clear of Stitch," Lincoln said, stating the obvious but glad to get it out of the way.

"At least he hasn't risen to full power yet," Kayleigh mused.

"No, but that doesn't mean he's not dangerous. Even without Ka Tolerates inside of him."

Kayleigh set her glass aside and leaned back on her arms. "So what do you think about Mona? She looks and sounds like our Mona, but this time difference confuses everything."

"And this Trokamano Pandiment. Taira Han didn't say anything about it. Neither did Creek. It sounds just as important as the Pandiment of Time, though now we can't even give that to ourselves because the blind sisters are dead."

"Yeah, that's not good news."

The sky just above the orchard was tinted with a soft dust of orange embers. Night was descending from above. Kayleigh wondered which direction the apiary Mona had spoken of was. Leaning over, she rested her head on his shoulder.

"It feels like we're in the right place," Lincoln said, "I'm just not sure where to go next."

17

"Isn't it obvious?" Kayleigh said, yawning. "We have to go to the place where this all started."

"But the Oak Hotel hasn't been built yet."

"Maybe not, but there's got to be something at the top of that mountain. We'll find it tomorrow."

Lincoln cringed at the memory of having Kayleigh taken from him, of losing her with no hope of return. If I could take her back to Autumn Harbor and continue this on my own, he thought (not for the first time), I would. The idea of walking into yet another trap nagged at the back of his mind. Creek's words about something horrible awaiting them would not let go. Instead of voicing this fear, he closed his eyes and sighed.

"Tomorrow, then," he said.

2. Mount Aikona

ayleigh awoke first, breathing in the dream-like aroma of the orchard through half-open windows. With care, she quietly padded to the front door and let herself out onto the porch. A cool breeze wound through the tree covered hills and with it came a faint, yet audible snapping sound. Walking down the steps onto the main drive, she soon learned the origin of the sound. A team of pruners were busy at a nearby copse of overgrown trees. They wore thick, scratchy-looking overalls and knelt expertly beneath the young trees. Reaching up with long, orange-tipped shears, they carefully pared away branches until, as time passed, the trees took on a uniform shape. Walking back up onto the porch, Kayleigh looked out and noticed several other teams of pruners working in seemingly random spots throughout the hills. A bit further in the distance, over the nearest rise, came the familiar sound of a train whistle. Cotton-thick tufts of smoke lifted with grudging ease into the morning sky just over the treetops.

"I often sit out here in the morning," Mona said, startling Kayleigh. The old woman moved to one of several rocking chairs and set herself down onto it. "I love the orchard at first light."

Kayleigh considered sitting in the rocker beside her, but decided to stand.

"Mona," she said. "Yesterday, when you told us about the fortunes the girls gave you, they said that Lincoln and I would tell you what needs to be done."

"That's right," Mona said softly, eyes focused on some distant point over the hills.

"But we don't know what needs to be done. The Oak Hotel needs to be built, but I guess that's obvious. We need to see the three sisters, but they're dead, so that's out. I just feel like we've come all this way and nothing makes sense."

Mona smiled up at her and said, "Dear one, I hear your words. I have lived my life feeling as you do, as if some important bit of information is just outside my grasp. But now, two special young people have entered my life and I know that things are going to be fine."

"But how can you know that?" Kayleigh asked, her fingers digging into her palms.

"It's not about knowing, but feeling."

The door opened and Lincoln stepped out with a thin, grey towel draped over his shoulder. Kayleigh nearly jumped to her feet and ran to him. He thought she was about to throw her arms around him in a hug, but instead she leaned into him and gently set her cheek against his. She took a deep breath.

"You washed your hair?" she asked in shock, pulling back.

"My hair and the rest of me, too. I found the wash tub in that little room off the kitchen. The tub was filled with warm water so I—"

Kayleigh spun and looked at Mona.

Smiling wider, Mona nodded, "Go ahead, Kayleigh. Rylyn has already drained the tub and refilled it with water for you."

Kayleigh literally danced back into the farmhouse.

Shaking his head, Lincoln asked, "What's gotten into her?"

"Lincoln, when was the last time either of you bathed?"

His eyes rose skyward for a moment, then returned to earth. "Probably back in Ceca Hebona," he said.

"And how long ago was that?"

Lincoln frowned.

"That's what I thought," Mona smiled.

After a glorious lunch with bowls of rapture figs and sweet cream for dessert, Mona called for Rylyn, who was busying herself about the kitchen. Kayleigh had been watching the older girl since they arrived and was impressed with how much she knew about the orchard.

Rylyn shyly sat down between Mona and Lincoln, smoothing out the fabric of her homespun apron.

"Rylyn, I was wondering if you could help us out," Mona said.

"Of course," was her reply.

"How well do you know the young man who helped to install that new cable train?" Mona asked with a subtle smile.

Rylyn blushed. "You mean Godfray? He's Goodman Hannum's oldest son. He and his family won't start their harvest for another month, so his father let him join the

SkyCar team. He said the new Mayor would pay them all well for their services."

"I see…" Mona said off-handedly. "So… this *SkyCar* is finished then?"

"I believe so," Rylyn added.

"If you asked Godfray, might he allow our friends Kayleigh and Lincoln here to make a quick trip up to the top of Mount Aikona?"

Rylyn thought for a moment, then tilted her head just a bit and smirked at Mona. "It just so happens that Godfray is in the orchard this morning helping Mr. Keage with the pruning."

"Oh," Mona said with mock surprise, "So he is! I suppose it wouldn't take a few minutes for you to go out and ask him right now."

"Certainly," Rylyn smiled, then turned to Kayleigh and Lincoln. "I am sorry if I scared you unnecessarily with Mona's impending death yesterday."

"My dear," Mona stepped in, before Kayleigh or Lincoln could say a word, "I accept all the responsibility for my actions, including what I asked you do to for me. It is I who should apologize to you."

Rylyn looked down at her feet for a moment, then glanced up shyly. "I'll go speak with Godfray."

"Thank you, dear," Mona said with a genuine smile.

About an hour later, Kayleigh and Lincoln (accompanied by Rylyn and Godfray Hannum) were walking east on the inner side of the train tracks.

"Can't we just take the train?" Lincoln asked.

"'Tis quicker this way," said Godfray, who had been quiet up until then. "The BTEL circles the woodlands in one direction until it connects to the older Western Line, but both trains are in the Round House for upkeep until noon. A third train is planned for the end of the month."

"I'd rather walk anyway," Kayleigh said, truly enjoying the afternoon.

Lincoln, struggling with the straps of his backpack (trying to keep the heavy load from coming loose) reached out and pulled Kayleigh slowly back toward him.

"I don't like this," he whispered.

"Why? It's amazing when you think about it. I'd love to go back in time back to see Autumn Harbor."

"That's not what I mean," he countered. "It's Stitch. I don't want to be anywhere near him, even if he doesn't know who we are yet. I feel like he's going to jump out from behind a bush—"

"And take me?" Kayleigh smiled.

"How can you think that's funny?"

She punched him lightly on the shoulder, which loosened one of the straps and sent his backpack sliding off his shoulder. "It's not funny," Kayleigh said. "I'm just glad I have you to look out for me."

At this point, Lincoln's backpack tipped completely over and the cord binding the flap at the top pulled open, spilling the contents in a heap on the ground between them.

Rylyn and Godfray turned.

"Don't worry about us," Kayleigh said with a calculating smile. "You two go on ahead. We'll catch up."

Visibly liking this advice, Godfray encouraged Rylyn to continue on with him. Rylyn shot one final glance back at them before growing smaller down the tracks.

Ignoring all other items, Lincoln fussed over a clear, foot-long cylinder.

"Did it crack?" Kayleigh asked, kneeling down with him.

"I don't think so. Who knows... it looks like glass, but it might be something stronger." He touched the heliodex and observed the hundreds of small, green acorns packed snugly within it. "Are you sure we should be taking this with us?"

"Might as well. We've gone back in time, but who knows how or when we might see my Grandfather again."

"What about Kafír? Do you think she's here, in this time?"

"I've been thinking about that, too. We should probably make that our next stop."

Filling the empty pack with dented boxes of Pop Top Taffy and crumpled wax paper wrapped balls of popcorn (courtesy of Shipmaster Creek), they made a comfortable nest for the heliodex.

In less than an hour, they caught up with Rylyn and Godfray at the newly constructed platform just before a shiny SkyCarOne.

"It seems as out of place now as it does in our time," Lincoln said, running an outstretched palm against the cool, metallic hull.

"Borrowed technology," Kayleigh added quietly.

"Truly," Godfray said, excited at the opportunity to add to the conversation. "SkyCarOne was built from designs Mayor Stitch brought from far away. Possibly Deep Traders."

"*Deep* Traders?" Kayleigh asked.

"Traders who have traveled not only from other worlds, but times."

"Sounds like us," Lincoln murmured, smiling.

"A true marvel, it is!" Godfray said, stepping up and opening the door.

Kayleigh and Lincoln stepped in, but Rylyn held her arm out as Godfray followed. "Mona wishes for them to visit the top alone," she explained as the blast from one of the distant trains filled the air. "We can ride the Line together if you'd like," she said innocently.

Godfray straightened. "I would be honored to help you in any way possible."

Kayleigh laughed as she sat on the narrow bench inside the slightly rocking car. "I think Rylyn would be happy just to have you sit beside her on the train."

Godfray's brow creased as if trying to discern the meaning of her words.

"Have fun guys," Lincoln said and pulled the door closed. "Yikes," he continued, "Can't he see that she likes him?" He sat beside Kayleigh.

"I think he likes her," she said, reaching out and pressing in the small button marked UP.

At once, the conveyance came to life and began its slow, but certain upward ascent.

When Kayleigh stepped onto the mountaintop, she gasped. Lincoln jumped at her quick intake of breath and nearly stumbled as he stepped out of SkyCarOne.

The Oak Hotel was missing. They knew this and expected it, but the fact that it was not there caused them both to feel uneasy.

Lincoln walked slowly toward the missing front entrance. "I feel... I don't know. All mixed up? Sad and dizzy and scared and—"

"Lonely," Kayleigh added, moving toward the area where the back staircase had once (would one day) climb up the rear of the majestic building. "And mad."

Turning toward her, Lincoln's eyes widened. "Its like someone died. Someone important."

"Yes," Kayleigh hissed, holding back tears and feeling foolish for such wild and unbidden emotions. She shuffled quickly back to where Lincoln stood and took both his hands in hers.

"This is crazy," she said, "But I feel like picking up a hammer and building it right now. It should be here. It should always be here. This empty space is wrong and it makes me feel sick inside."

"We're more a part of all this than we thought," Lincoln whispered. Walking to the eastern edge of the bluff, he sank to his knees and ran his hands over the ground. Kayleigh joined him.

"There were pine trees when we first came to this place," Lincoln said.

"They were small pines," Kayleigh said softly. "Young trees. They must have come much later."

"I think I still have—" Lincoln's voice trailed off. Reaching into his pocket, he withdrew the acorn he'd found on the ground near the remains of Kafír Rosette.

Kayleigh raised her eyes. "We really are supposed to be here."

Afraid to smile, afraid to breathe, Lincoln knelt down and dug his shaky fingers into a patch of warm, exposed soil. When he had created a six-inch hole, he rolled the acorn into the bottom and slowly pushed the loose earth back over it. His body seemed to hum as he stood and turned toward Kayleigh.

"I was supposed to do that," he said.

"Yes," she replied, "But... do you remember an oak tree growing here back in our time?"

Lincoln frowned. "No. I don't remember seeing an oak tree anywhere on this mountain."

"So there must be another reason."

That reason caused them both to jump in shock as a six-foot high oval portal opened in the air just above the place where the acorn lay. Inside the shape, complex geometries danced to the grace of unheard music. It was pure darkness inspired by transformations just out of the range of human sight. Of course, Kayleigh and Lincoln had seen portals like this before.

"We didn't use a Pandiment," Lincoln said, feeling himself drawn ever closer toward the waiting doorway.

Kayleigh tried to speak, but her mouth and throat were dry.

"Who's doing this?" Lincoln asked, wishing he could take back his question.

Kayleigh felt a disturbing tug at her mind and body. She wanted to respond to it, but something caused her to resist. There wasn't anything physically wrong with the portal, compared to the other times they'd used one. This time, however, it appeared stronger. More powerful.

Lincoln moved to her side so that their shoulders were pressed together. Kayleigh immediately took his hand and squeezed hard. Lincoln's words came out in a jumbled rush: "This is what it felt like when we stood near Ka Tolerates. It was forcing me to get closer to it. It tried to get into my mind."

Exactly, thought Kayleigh. She pressed a thought (a question) through the portal with her mind: *Who are you and what do you want with us?*

The voice that filled her mind drained every last bit of worry and fear. It was a cool sip of something fizzy and sweet on a summer day. It said:

Come to me, Kayleigh Kell-Korai. Come to me, Queen of the Oaks.

Taking a deep, shuddering breath, Kayleigh said, "We're going through."

Lincoln wanted to scream. He squeezed his eyes tightly shut.

There was no time to be delicate. With a vice-grip on Lincoln's hand, Kayleigh pulled him with her. In three quick strides, they pushed through the soft, yielding membrane of the portal.

3. The Last Oak Tree

The only thing that passed through Lincoln's panicked mind was the anticipation of pain. Although lessened on his last trip through the portal at the top of the Painted Lighthouse, he still braced himself for the hot explosion of torn nerves.

But there was nothing.

Instead, he and Kayleigh stepped onto moss-soft ground. Their sneaker clad feet made not a sound as their eyes adjusted to the dim light. They appeared to have come out in the middle of a forest. Tall, imposing trees reached mightily upward, creating a ceiling of leaves and branches high above. Spaced evenly in long, straight rows, they created a natural path.

"I knew we should have gone to see Kafír. She probably sent the portal for us," Lincoln whispered.

Kayleigh said nothing, but led them down the widest path toward what appeared to be (far in the distance) an open field.

Though the sky above was shielded by green, light was slowly making its way through. The grey and powdery twilight behind them was strengthening to the warm beginning of morning's blush.

Without turning, Kayleigh said, "It didn't hurt for you to go through this time?"

"Uh, no," Lincoln replied, sprinting a bit to keep up with her.

"Why?" she asked.

Matching her quick pace, he said, "I don't know."

"The portal we stepped through was huge," he said, not smiling.

"It follows the rules, at least as far as we know the rules," Lincoln offered. "A portal can only appear where a de'Malange stands or once stood, right? Well, I planted that acorn in the ground. That counts, right?"

"This portal was different, though. More… real. I don't know how to describe it."

"You don't think Kafîr made the portal?"

This time, Kayleigh chuckled, "No. This has nothing to do with Kafîr. This is something—".

At that moment, the first tentative rays of morning sunlight crested the distant, unseen horizon behind them. Looking up, they saw the leaves at the very tops of the trees light as if on fire. A strong wind pushed down through the trees.

And then: the glory and majesty and heartache of music broke above and around them. It was unlike any music either had ever heard. It filled their hearts to bursting. There were no words, only pure emotion as hundreds of voices moved in and between the rise and fall of distant, oceanic waves.

Lincoln pulled Kayleigh impulsively to him. Looking back down at him, her eyes proved that she was as totally enthralled with the sound as he was. He leaned close, needing to be near her. They were so close, in fact, that their lips almost touched as if in a tentative kiss. There was no room for words or explanation. He just knew that being this close to her was *right* and it sent his heart racing even faster.

Saying nothing in reply, she smiled, closed her eyes and they embraced, allowing the rising, complex harmonics to carry them to a higher place.

In Kayleigh's mind, the strange voice said:

It is true that your fate is intricately entwined with his, but you must come to me now. It is not far.

"Lincoln," Kayleigh whispered. "We need to go."

The trees around them shimmered in the growing light as the music reached its mysterious climax. Lincoln's eyes were alight as he asked:

"Is this the Symphony of Dawn that Emil told us about? Are we on Te'hæra Thorn?"

"Yes."

"Did the de'Malange send for us? Did they create the portal?"

"Well… *one* of them did. She's calling for us. We need to go."

And so, without further words, the two friends walked quickly and eventually ran down the path between the trees, carried on by promise of the trees.

Morning was full upon the world by the time they exited the Valley of the Oaks. The Symphony of Dawn had ended in a brilliant finale. Lincoln didn't feel as if he were being watched, but rather *listened* to. It was overwhelming enough being in the presence of Kafîr Rosette, one de'Malange oak, but an entire forest of them!

Kayleigh could only stare at the small oak ahead of them. It grew at the base of a rise of land they both immediately recognized. Beyond this hill waited the great red city of Kana Hove, home to the Pilgrims who journeyed across the vastness of space to escape the tyranny of Atoth.

"Whoa, wait a minute," Lincoln said, finally realizing where they were now going. "That tree—"

Kayleigh slowed and they were now walking across the mossy ground.

"—that's…" and here, he whispered, "Ka Tolerates."

Without turning toward him, Kayleigh shook her head. "Not the Ka Tolerates we knew."

"But that's the tree Truman touched. All these other de'Malange were gone. Emil told us they'd been cut down."

"Shhh…" was Kayleigh's only reply as they closed the distance between themselves and the lone oak.

Twenty feet from the tree was as far as Lincoln could force himself to go. Kayleigh continued on and stepped up to the nearly miniature (at least, compared to the other de'Malange) tree. She stepped up and embraced it, wrapping her arms as far as they would go around the trunk.

Something in Lincoln broke and tears welled in his eyes. He could not, at first, explain why. An uncontrolled sob wracked his chest and he fell to his knees. Alarmed at this total loss of control, Lincoln began to cry freely, fearing he'd completely lost his mind.

Do not fear me, dear one, a motherly voice spoke to him. He knew at once it came from this tree, but didn't the de'Malange speak when the wind passed over their leaves and branches?

Yes, the voice chuckled. *We can speak in that manner, but usually only to sing. Your special friend, Kafir, never learned to speak as I now do.*

Kayleigh stepped back and placed her open palms gently upon the trunk.

At long last, you have come to us, Queen of the Oaks, the tree said to her.

Kayleigh turned to Lincoln, who nodded. "I can hear it, too," he said.

Laughter filled their minds. Laughter suffused with a happiness neither had ever thought possible.

"We were here," Kayleigh said quietly. "When Stitch touched you."

"You were horrible," Lincoln said, swallowing. "Are you—?"

Yes, the tree spoke, *I am Ka Tolerates. It saddens me to know that you harbor such dark memories. What happened to me and all that you know is in my future.*

"We traveled back in time through a door in the Painted Lighthouse," Kayleigh said, sitting now with her back against the tree. She stared at Lincoln.

"We must have just traveled backward in time again," he said.

Yes.

"How far back?" Kayleigh asked.

I am not certain of the exact time in years. Thousands of your years, at least. We have brought you back to the time and place of the great exodus. All of the de'Malange, except myself (of course) will soon leave this lonely planet.

"Are the Pilgrims from Atoth still in Kana Hove?" Lincoln asked.

Indeed, they are.

Kayleigh stood quickly. "We have to go now!" she began. "My Grandfather's alive in this time. He's in the city! This is the only way can deliver the heliodex to him."

Calm yourself. Of course, what you say is exactly what we planned upon. You will leave me for a short time and deliver the heliodex to Emil, but...

It was strange to hear the tree's voice pause.

"Oh," Kayleigh said, now standing beside Lincoln. "I get it. We can't say anything about what happens to *you*, or about my Grandfather getting killed."

Yes, but moreover, you cannot allow Emil to even see you. What has happened in your past and my future must still happen. Although Stitch is a strange and, frankly, unforeseen free radical in our narrative, he now must be dealt with. And you two will be the ones who bring him to justice.

"Um, we were hoping," Lincoln began, "That once he went back to Atoth, the people there would take care of him. From what we've learned, I'm not sure they're happy with him for how things turned out."

The voice inside their heads grew slightly dark when it replied:

Trust me when I say that the Applewhites will not view Stitch's failure in a positive light. He will be punished. The technology on Atoth will allow the reigning family to exile him permanently. He will no longer be of any threat to anyone.

"That's good, then, right?" Kayleigh asked. "Why do we need to bring him to justice if he's already getting what he deserves?"

Because, our dear Queen, Stitch has something important... something we need if our mission is to succeed.

"About that," Lincoln interrupted hesitantly. "Are we ever going to find out what this mission is?"

When you have successfully delivered the heliodex, I will answer your questions and explain what still needs to be done. At no point, however, are you to interact with Emil. It is imperative that he know nothing of your visit. Now, please, you must go...

Upon leaving Ka Tolerates and the valley, Lincoln felt as if the hundreds of trees were crouching expectantly in anticipation. The two suns were almost directly above them now, but the weather was mild—a day in mid-autumn.

"So how are we going to make sure he knows how important the heliodex is without giving it to him ourselves?" Lincoln asked.

Kayleigh shook her head and breathed out slowly, "I'm more worried about finding someone we can trust to give it to him."

Cresting the hill, the red city came into view. If it had appeared grand and mysterious on their first visit, Kana Hove now overwhelmed them with its grandeur. It reminded Kayleigh of pictures she'd seen of St. Basil's Cathedral in Moscow. Kana Hove, however, was a sprawling city's worth of striped domes, both tall and plump. Vaulted towers rose at seemingly random intervals among the hip-capped spires. And all constructed from the same translucent, scarlet stone.

They reached the main gate, marveling at the orderly movement of people as they made their way between doorways and arches. This was another stark difference from their first visit, where Emil had been the city's sole inhabitant.

"These are your people," Lincoln said softly in an awed tone, "The Pilgrims from Atoth."

Kayleigh only nodded, watching their casual, yet purposeful stride. Each wore slightly baggy pants and a top that resembled a poncho. The fabric composing these garments was a washed-out red, lighter than the buildings surrounding them. As they entered the main courtyard, both were amazed that not one of the city's inhabitants looked shocked or surprised to see them there. Obviously, Kayleigh and Lincoln were outsiders, but each man and woman that gave any notice offered only smiles or silent nods of greeting.

"It's like they know why we're here," Kayleigh said.

A low, electric shock filled Lincoln at her words, but he knew that she was right. The trees must have already communicated what was happening. They might have known all along what was going to happen…

Before they even had the chance to comment further, a short woman with shoulder-length grey hair appeared between them and gracefully slid her hands between their arms.

"Greetings my young ones," she said in a warm, dry voice. "We must get you inside."

With a gentle tug forward, she led them between an unending progression of majestic buildings until, finally, they stopped before a familiar site.

"The Tower of Quercus," Kayleigh said, looking up at the tallest structure in Kana Hove.

The old woman let go of Lincoln's arm and laced all her dry, frail fingers into Kayleigh's. "I have forgotten that this is not your first visit."

"We came here… at a future time," Kayleigh said.

She turned to Lincoln, "And were you here as well?"

"Yes," Lincoln said, barely getting the word past his lips. Something about this entire situation felt dreamlike—as if this meeting was meant to happen (was destined to happen), yet each word and breath vibrated on the finest thread threatening to break. Kayleigh looked into his eyes and he knew she felt the same way. Licking his lips and clearing his throat a bit, Lincoln looked back at the small figure.

"Emil took us into this building," he began. "He used the… vision beads and showed us how you and the others traveled here from Atoth. He was the only person left in the whole city."

"Except for Ka Tolerates," Kayleigh added, though wished she could have taken it back. The woman cast a quick, nervous glance around. With a look of determination, she led them quickly through the narrow archway into the silent Tower of Quercus.

4. Crossing Paths

These things," she whispered as they entered the privacy of the tower, "Should not be spoken of lightly."

"But my Grandfather was alone. He was abandoned." Kayleigh felt an old anger stirring within her. "We know that he will wake up one morning and discover the city empty and all of the trees gone. Ka Tolerates—"

But the woman was no longer listening, having moved ahead of them into the main room. As it had been on their previous visit, the pool of tiny glass spheres sat recessed in the center of the floor. Also, the familiar door with the acorn at its center sat closed on the opposite side of the room.

"Come," she said, sitting before the silent collection of beads, "What I have to tell you is vital. Sit with me, please."

Kayleigh walked toward her, but Lincoln stood still and smiled. Inspired, he chanced a guess. "You're Kayleigh's Grandmother, Laura Corwin."

Kayleigh's eyes widened with shock.

The woman's look of impatience turned at once to consternation. "My name is Pearle Kho. Laura Corwin has not yet been born and Emil has not left this planet since his arrival. Back on Atoth, my parents were members of the Royal Family Kel-Rhodanic. Our family had strong ties to the Kell-Korai clan. For what it's worth, Kayleigh, you and I are related by many links in our heritage."

Pearle closed her eyes and rested two open palms on her crossed legs as Emil had done. "I am the only surviving member of my family. If it hadn't been for Emil, I would be dead as well. I fear that we here in Kana Hove are the only ones of the true blood who remain."

Lincoln thought about mentioning his own family's flight and settling near Burnam Tau'roh, but just as he took a breath to speak, tens of thousands of tiny glass beads rushed into the space above the bowl. The strange sound they made was familiar and, both Kayleigh and Lincoln were surprised to discover, welcoming. The blurred vision before them went from a hypnotic, undulating sphere of grey to an icy black.

Pearle's voice, stronger now, filled the room as an image began to solidify within the now silent bead cloud:

"Truman Stitch has been punished for his crimes against humanity. In your time, he left de'Na for Atoth. He thought he had you, Kayleigh, as a trophy to mend his reputation with the Applewhites. It was soon discovered that he had failed in every way possible. When Sirnaq Applewhite found that the *ghesthi'voult* (the negative energy the de'Malange had taken from us) was intermingled with Stitch's soul, he was furious. And concerned. He commissioned a group to discover or manufacture an inescapable prison."

As she spoke, images passed before them. They saw Truman Stitch standing before a tribunal of elders. Each face was grave and condemning. They watched as Truman was taken away and held against a dull, silver wall with some sort of shimmering force field. In another room, the same group of ancient faces sat conferring over what to do with him.

46

"What kind of jail did they put him in?" Lincoln asked.

As if in answer to his query, Sirnaq Applewhite (a tall, thin man with white hair and chin-length beard) stood from his seat and spoke to the gathered: "It is agreed upon that no prison on our world is capable of permanently holding the abomination that Truman Stitch has become. Therefore, we must look elsewhere."

The scene shifted in a quick right-to-left blur of light and they saw Applewhite again, though in less formal attire. He stood in a dark corridor beside a young male not much older than Lincoln.

"Is that David?" Kayleigh asked aloud.

Lincoln couldn't speak. The boy standing there was definitely his newfound brother, David Grey.

"Are you certain it's possible?" Applewhite asked. "You can fix things to accomplish the transfer."

"Yes," David replied, visibly intimidated by the man he stood before. "But..."

"Yes?"

"Sending him there... would break every one of your laws."

Applewhite smiled darkly, then settled his arm gently on David's shoulders. "As intelligent as you are, my boy, there is much yet for you to learn."

The two moved down the hallway into darkness. Pearle's voice resumed:

"This is the only intelligence we have on where Stitch was sent. They kept the details quiet, even among themselves. It's probable that Sirnaq and David Grey are the only ones who know of the location of this prison. Furthermore, it's possible that David alone knows the exact details."

In one dissonant hush, the beads lost coherence and fell into the depression below.

Pearle opened her eyes.

"I don't get it," Kayleigh began, staring at the woman's troubled face. "This is a good thing, right? If Stitch is gone forever, then he can't hurt anyone. Back in Burnam Tau'roh, when Stitch left, they celebrated!"

Pearle's brow creased further, "Things are a bit more complicated, child. When Stitch touches the tree, he will absorb every last negative thought of each person here in Kana Hove."

"Yeah," Lincoln said, shifting uncomfortably, "We sort of stood there while it happened."

Pearle blanched. "Indeed," she said. "Then you will understand what I'm about to say with more depth than I imagined. Stitch not only absorbed the purest of negative energy, but Ka Tolerates' *sáwol*, or eternal spirit, as well. The de'Malange have just recently let us know that soon a time will come when we must all leave our physical bodies and join them on a great journey. This cannot happen, however, unless we are all present."

"Except for my Grandfather," Kayleigh said.

"His body is (will be) gone, this is true, but Emil Kell-Korai's *sáwol* will live on inside of Stitch. Your Grandfather's strong will is the only thing keeping Ka Tolerates from being destroyed within the warped and twisted mind of Truman Stitch. Whatever the de'Malange have planned for our journey, it cannot continue unless we are reunited with both Ka Tolerates and Emil Kell-Korai."

"And now there's no hope of getting them back," Kayleigh added. "Unless we can find where Stitch was imprisoned."

"With all the resources available to us, I am saddened to admit that this one piece of important information is missing from a very complicated equation."

Standing, Kayleigh started to pace the area between the bead pool and the archway. "I'm sure there's a reason for this and I don't mean to sound ignorant, but why can't we just go to my Grandfather right now and tell him what's going to happen? Won't he understand? I'm sure he can think of some way around this."

"It's not a matter of simple understanding," Pearle said patiently. "If Emil knew his place in all of this, he would agree that it would be best not to know his own future. Besides, this confusion of past, present and future is why we must all tread lightly. The two of you are as entangled in the de'Malange tapestry as Emil. Would you be willing to jeopardize your success by acting on information that would alter the outcome?"

Kayleigh and Lincoln glanced at each other.

It was then that Pearle Kho laughed. The sound surprised them, but in a good way. It lightened the moment; her next comment, however, quickly brought reality down upon them.

"Ah, please excuse me. My old way of thinking often clouds what I've known to be true. Since we've met the de'Malange, we see things like time in a different way. The fact remains, you cannot change things. Or, to do so would be exceedingly difficult. And by exceedingly, I mean near impossible."

"Then changing the course of history is exactly what they are trying to do, then, isn't it?" Kayleigh asked, a smile of her own playing across her face. Lincoln stared at her and thought, as he had been doing more and more often since their entry into these strange worlds, how startlingly beautiful she was. Kayleigh continued: "Stitch may have done something wrong, something evil, but it's really the de'Malange who are trying to alter things."

Pearle moved toward Kayleigh and embraced her. Lincoln watched as Kayleigh first stood rigid in surprise, then softened and returned the hug. Pearle took a step back and stared into Kayleigh's eyes. "You are truly the one they have been speaking of, Queen of the Oaks."

"I don't think such a royal title belongs to me," Kayleigh said, cheeks reddening. "If anything, Ka Tolerates should be Queen of the Oaks."

Still smiling, Pearle said softly, "It was Ka Tolerates who first spoke this title in reference to you, child."

"I know I'm part of an important family, but I just don't see why it's all landing on *me*," Kayleigh whispered.

Pearle took her hand and said in mild amusement, "I am certain these same words have been uttered by nearly every young member of a royal family. Especially just before they are to take the throne and accept their own crown."

From outside, the sweet sound of a distant bell rang, filling the mid-afternoon with gold.

"You haven't much time left here," Pearle said, motioning for Lincoln to join them. "I shall be the one to pass the heliodex to Emil. He will know nothing of your involvement or that you were even here."

"So there's nothing we can do to save him?" Kayleigh asked, shaking her head at the craziness of just letting him move closer and closer to his death.

Lincoln knelt to the floor and was rummaging through his pack for the heliodex.

"If it were possible to do what you say," Pearle spoke quickly, "Emil would not leave Kana Hove in search of us, never discover Earth, never meet your Grandmother and you, my dear Kayleigh, would never be born. There are simply too many what-ifs. The delicacy in the balance of what is now happening is beyond anything I can describe to you."

Finding the reinforced glass cylinder, Lincoln stood and held it out. Pearle accepted it, marveling at the chocolaty-brown acorns packed safely within.

"I don't know either of your spiritual beliefs, children, but what this all comes down to is faith that you are a part of something good. Something wonderful."

The bell stopped tolling.

"Alright," Pearle spoke, even faster now, "Follow me. I will lead you safely from our city back to the Valley. Ka Tolerates will speak with you before you go."

They moved quickly, tracing a circuitous route toward the archway at the entrance of Kana Hove. Pearle pointed them down toward the crest of a hill.

"Well," she said, giving them each a quick embrace. "If everything goes the way it should, I'll see you again. Good luck."

With that, she turned and walked quickly back toward the red city. The sun above was beginning its downward arc and a sweet-scented breeze pushed gently against them.

Taking her hand in his, and never imagining he'd ever tire of holding it, Lincoln took the first step that led them down again toward the valley.

"So," Kayleigh said, trying to organize what they'd just heard in her mind, "The de'Malange are planning on some great voyage, but they need everyone (all the oaks and all the Pilgrims) in order to do it."

"But," Lincoln said, "they can't do this because both Ka Tolerates and Emil are trapped inside Truman Stitch, who has been imprisoned in some unknown location."

Kayleigh sighed. "I really wish we could just turn around and talk to my Grandfather. What Pearle said makes sense, kind of, but I think he'd know what to do."

They walked a bit further when Lincoln said, "I wish I could talk with my parents."

Kayleigh said nothing. A sharp twinge filled her chest at the thought of her own parents. If only they could send some sort of message back to them, just to let them know she and

Lincoln were still alive. She also wondered, too, if her parents (well, her Mom at least) secretly knew anything about Emil and his origins.

They crossed the expanse between the city and valley and slowed as they approached Ka Tolerates. Without acknowledging the feeling, both shuddered at the memory of walking the same steps to a future, blackened version of this tree. The sound it made, combined with the image of coal-black branch-arms writhing in the air, were difficult to forget.

Dear ones, the ancient oak spoke, her voice now sweet and without hint of malice. *Again, I am sorry you carry these memories of me. It was not my true self, but a sacrifice I had to make in order that the others make their transformation.*

"You don't sound very upset about what's going to happen to you," Kayleigh said, kneeling with Lincoln before the tree on a bed of moss and clover.

The sacrifices we make are neither great nor small. They are, instead, testimony to our belief in... kindness. Integrity. Honesty. I have faith that the Atoth Pilgrims will, when the time comes, join us.

"You're going on a great journey," Lincoln said.

The leaves of the tree before them seemed to shiver, though there was no breeze.

Yes, the de'Malange breathed. *A voyage unlike any other we've already taken. A crossing of impossible magnitude. From our humble beginnings, we are close to completing the final stage of our magnum opus.*

"Are we going on this journey with you?" Kayleigh asked, wishing she could take the question back.

Ka Tolerates paused before answering.

In the end, one of you will make the journey with us. I cannot say more, for there are elements still in darkness. Your life on Earth has been taken from you. If it helps to place the blame, then put it on me. I will not lie when I say that a greater test awaits you. Stitch must be found at all costs. Emil and I must be returned.

The sun was nearly down and the breeze, which had by then become constant, grew in strength.

We will be singing again soon. It is time you returned to our dear Mona Tarok, but first there is a favor I must ask of you both. It is something you will find distasteful, but something, ultimately, that must be accomplished if we are to continue our journey.

Now, pay careful attention...

5. Grand Endeavor

ayleigh and Lincoln stepped back through the portal to the sorrowful rapture of The Symphony of Dusk. When they had moved fully away from the green-black rotation, the doorway sprung back as if liquid-elastic then spiraled in upon itself and closed.

"I feel like…" Kayleigh began, then stopped. She could not find the words and her hands were shaking.

"Me, too," Lincoln said. The voice of Ka Tolerates, which had filled his mind as she explained exactly what needed to be done, left traces. It was as if he could still hear her talking, or whispering, even though their connection had been severed.

Without speaking, they moved quickly across the barren plateau of Mount Aikona toward the silver gleam of SkyCarOne. When they reached the small platform at the bottom, Rylyn and Godfray were walking toward them from the familiar Ticket Station IX on the other side of the tracks. They wore looks of concern and Rylyn graduated from a fast walk to a jog.

"Is everything alright?" Rylyn asked.

"Yes," Kayleigh said, confused. "Are you two okay?"

Godfray looked up to the mountain and then back to them. "I think we thought that, perhaps, you might have taken a bit longer."

"We've been gone for… what?" Lincoln asked, glancing at Kayleigh. Was the length of a day on Te'hæra Thorn that different from here in Burnam Tau'roh. "Six? Seven hours?"

"At least," Kayleigh said, but a thought came to her: Ka Tolerates must have sent us back only shortly after they left. Virtually no time had passed on this side of the portal.

"You know what?" Kayleigh smiled. "Why don't you two just go on as if we never came back down. We'll probably just explore around here for a while then head back to the orchard."

Rylyn's eyebrows narrowed. Kayleigh felt a pang of guilt at not being able to tell her what they knew, especially considering that Rylyn would be playing an important part in all of this, too. Lincoln picked up on this as well, adding, "Aren't you and Mona going to show us how you preserve the rapture figs later this evening?"

Rylyn looked to Lincoln, then back to Kayleigh and seemed to understand.

"Of course," she said, "I'll meet you back at the orchard in a few hours."

Leaving their slightly confused friend behind, they followed the tracks back to the road leading to Trokamano Orchard. They entered the house, but could not find Mona anywhere. Calling out did not bring her around and after ten further minutes of searching they began to worry.

Sitting in the kitchen, they were prepared to search the orchard and question the workers when they heard a faint voice calling out, "Kayleigh? Lincoln? Have you returned already?"

Jumping up, they followed the direction of Mona's voice to the rear of the kitchen. There, behind a thick, thatch curtain they hadn't noticed earlier, was a dark passage leading down.

"Mona?" Kayleigh called.

"Down here, dears!" the old woman's voice echoed hollowly.

There were nineteen stone steps leading down, each curving slightly to the left. At the bottom, they found a long, subterranean room. The ceiling was low, no higher than six feet, and the walls to the right and left were lined with an impossible collection of various sized jars filled with preserved fruit.

Sitting at a wide wooden desk at the far end of this amazing room was Mona. She turned to them as they approached.

"I didn't expect you back until dinner or later," she said, frowning.

"We've been gone for almost the entire day," Kayleigh said, noticing the large pile of leather-bound books sitting in a stack on the desk.

"Do you remember what we told you about Ka Tolerates?" Lincoln asked.

"You mean the evil tree that becomes part of Truman Stitch?" Mona answered, still with a note of disbelief.

"Yes," Lincoln said, "Well, it turns out that Ka Tolerates is kind of the leader of the de'Malange and after we spent the day in the Valley of the Oaks and Kana Hove, she sent us back here with some news none of us are really happy with."

Mona looked down at the desk.

"What are all those books for?" Kayleigh asked.

The older woman pulled one from the table and held it open toward them. The pages of the book were blank. "Truman Stitch had these delivered after you left. There are nineteen of them. Since I'm now the town chronicler, these will be my ledgers for recording things as they happen."

"You don't sound... thrilled about this new job," Lincoln offered.

"Well, young man, to be honest I don't know how to feel about any of this. I'm not a young lady like Rylyn or your sweet Kayleigh here. I feel as if I'm at the end of my own little story."

"But that can't be true," Kayleigh said. "We know you. Years from now, you help us and take care of the Oak Hotel."

"I understand all of that, dear," Mona said, "and I'm not saying I don't believe you."

Kayleigh sighed, attempting a small bit of business in her tone, "We have a few more things to tell you. You might have to stretch your imagination a bit further this time."

Setting the book she held back on the table, Mona turned her seat toward them and smiled. Kayleigh took a deep breath and began:

"You remember what we told you of the de'Malange oaks on the other planet? Well, in order for them to join their souls with the people of Kana Hove and continue this journey they're on, we have to cut down all of the trees."

Mona's eyes widened with shock.

"I know," Kayleigh continued. "I'm trying not to think about that part. Anyway, after we cut them down, we're supposed to bring the lumber to the top of Mount Aikona."

"The Oak Hotel," Mona breathed.

Lincoln stepped in, "We know that a portal will be opened to bring the trees through, but we don't know how it's all going to work out. Ka Tolerates said that you would probably know best how to organize the construction of the de'Malange wood into the frame of the hotel."

"Well, I am on the committee for the construction of the building, but we haven't met yet with our new Mayor. By the way, they're calling it the Burnam Tau'roh Hostel."

"When is the first committee meeting?" Kayleigh asked.

Smiling, Mona said, "Tomorrow morning at the Mayor's residence at GateHouse. I know this hotel is important. Mayor Stitch made it clear that he wants to bring as many people into

Burnam Tau'roh as possible. He wants this to become a *trading town*, as he put it."

"I'm sure he does," Lincoln said under his breath.

"Having a huge, contained area for traders to stay at makes sense," Kayleigh added, feeling a slight chill of satisfaction at finally seeing how things were beginning to fit together.

"After the meeting tomorrow, we'll have more information," Mona said. "Then we can start planning a bit more. When are you supposed to bring the trees through?"

"Lincoln asked about that," Kayleigh said, "but Ka Tolerates just said they would be ready when we were."

Mona turned back to the pile of new books. "It sounds like our sleepy little haven is going to get pretty busy," she breathed, then stood and turned back to the waiting pair. "Well, there's no reason we shouldn't start preparing for this grand endeavor now. Follow me, my dears."

She moved lithely past them toward the upward curve of stairs. Kayleigh and Lincoln followed without question. On the way up, Mona continued, "We still have a few hours of daylight left, so I'm sending you two on a little errand."

Kayleigh looked back at Lincoln, who smiled and said softly, "A *mini* adventure."

"Do you recall my mentioning Ben Tompkins and his honey? Well, before he got into bees, his family ran the largest lumber mill in Western Burnam Tau'roh."

"West?" Lincoln asked as they entered the kitchen. "I thought this area here was the western edge of Burnam Tau'roh."

"Oh, no," Mona said, "The Eastern and Western Railroads are connected by a long stretch of track that separates the entire province. It's not used much anymore. They used to called it Thunder Way. A hundred years ago, logging was the main industry and the West is where all the action was. They transported and sold their lumber in the shallow Western Sea. When the boom ended, most people spread out looking for work. A good number ended up here in the East."

They were now sitting where they had been yesterday upon first greeting Mona. It felt like story time all over again, Kayleigh thought.

"Alright, then. I'd like for you two to pay my good friend, Ben, a visit. It's been a while since I've been over there, but I'm sure he still has a barn full of tandem saws from the old logging days. You'll be needing saws for your upcoming venture, I suspect?"

Lincoln swallowed. Kayleigh forced a smile, not really looking forward to having to bring down even a single sentient tree. "Yes," Kayleigh said. "We'll need to be prepared."

Just then, three knocks on the front door.

"Excuse me," Mona said, rising from her seat. She shuffled the short distance across the room.

"Is it just me, or do you feel sick just thinking about cutting down those trees?" Lincoln asked.

Kayleigh paled. "I know. It feels like we're planning a murder or something."

They listened as Mona opened the door.

"Greetings, M. Tarok!" a loud, familiar voice boomed.

There was a momentary pause before Mona replied, "Why… good afternoon Mayor Stitch."

6. Bee Keepers

They were up in an instant with thoughts of running back to the hidden stairway and hiding among the preserves below, but the door swung wide and there was no escape.

Mona slid back as Stitch took two, wide steps into the narrow entry. He still hadn't walked far enough in, however, and Kayleigh and Lincoln were just out of sight behind the open door.

"I received the books," Mona said, trying her best to keep her voice from shaking. "They were delivered a few hours ago."

"Good. Nova Reckór was insistent upon posting you as chronicler and, forgive me, but she was getting on my nerves."

Mona found herself at a loss for words. Nova was a dear friend and one the most selfless people she knew. Hearing this stranger speak about her in such a way was almost too much.

Kayleigh wanted to take a step back and crouch down, but was afraid that the man beyond the door would sense movement.

"Being new to Burnam Tau'roh, I'm finding it difficult understanding its people and customs. You seem to know the families who have long had influence here and, additionally, have much influence and respect yourself. I would consider it… a great *favor* if you would agree to make our new hostel on the mountain your home once it is built."

Unable to stop herself, Mona turned to look directly at Kayleigh and Lincoln, who immediately nodded and pointed back through the door at the expectant mayor.

"Oh, of course," Mona stuttered, bringing her attention back to Stitch.

"I understand that you have an attachment to this orchard. You would retain it, of course. I can post anyone you wish to oversee it. It's just that I need someone I can trust to be my eyes and ears. I can trust you, M. Tarok, can I not?"

Not missing the importance of this minor exchange, Mona smiled and answered without pause, "I am here for you, Mayor Stitch."

"Good. That is exactly what I wanted to hear. You will be there tomorrow for the meeting."

"Yes."

"Until then, M. Tarok."

The door closed. No one moved until the retreating sound of hooves eventually turned to silence.

"That was crazy close," Lincoln said.

Mona turned and walked toward them. "This might sound strange," she said, "But part of me thinks he knew you were here. He was going to walk in, I felt it, but for some reason he just stopped. Given what you've told me, I get the feeling he knows we're all caught up in something beyond our control."

"When you were talking to him, I felt like I was standing on a cloud," Kayleigh said, letting out a breath. "And every second that passed, we were slowly falling through."

Mona shuddered, "You two should be off. Ben's not expecting you, but just tell him I sent you and he'll treat you like family. It's not far. You can get there quickest if you cut through the orchard. You'll end up on Long Reach Road. Just keep heading west and you'll see the sign for Tompkins Apiary. Can't miss it. Might take you an hour there and another back. You should be back before sunset."

"Good," Lincoln said. "There are still a few things we need to tell you, but Rylyn needs to be there, too. She's going to play an important part in all of this once the hotel is built."

Mona considered this. "Perhaps she'll be the one taking over here at the orchard when I'm gone."

Kayleigh and Lincoln said nothing, but hugged the old woman and left through the back door.

The journey through the orchard was uneventful, though pleasant. At one point, Lincoln bent down and picked up a stray rapture fig. He lifted the fruit to his nose to take in the wonderful aroma. Kayleigh jumped at him, knocking it from his hand in a frantic gesture.

"Jeez!" Lincoln said. "I wasn't going to eat it. I swear. I was just smelling it."

Kayleigh gave him a hard look. "I thought you forgot about it being poisonous until harvest time."

The disturbing truth was, Lincoln *had* forgotten this fact. What a mess things would have been had he bitten into the small, peach colored orb.

They passed only one worker who was tending a sickly looking tree. The lower limbs appeared oily and were covered with some sort of dark fungus. The young man snipped away at these branches with the pruners and dragged them to a pile a few feet away. He noticed them walking by, nodded a quick greeting then continued with his work. Lincoln couldn't help thinking of Ka Tolerates just after Stitch had touched it. Or Kafír Rosette after she'd been infected.

"Who do you think will take over here when Mona moves to the Oak Hotel?" Kayleigh asked, knowing that it definitely would not be Rylyn.

"I have no clue, but it's going to be hard for Mona to leave."

Kayleigh looked off to the north, watching frail clouds caress the rounded tops of the low mountains. "We should have told her about Rylyn."

"Ka Tolerates said we should tell them together."

"I know. It just feels strange holding it back."

Lincoln, who had somehow moved a few feet ahead of Kayleigh, stopped and let her catch up. "Everything is starting to change, you know. We finally know what's going on, at least more than before, and we're actually doing something about it."

"I don't know…" Kayleigh countered, but couldn't find the words to convey her uneasiness.

In less than a half-hour, they had crossed the entire orchard and stepped out onto Long Reach Road. Turning right onto it, they walked about a mile or so before stopping at a large wooden sign on their right:

TOMPKINS APIARY EAST

OLD BURNAM TAU'ROH BEE YARD

The ground crunched oddly beneath them as they moved up the narrow drive toward a beautiful, stone-faced house. Lincoln bent down and scooped up what appeared to be a handful of crushed seashells.

"Weird," he said, then let the pulverized pieces fall through his fingers and caught up with Kayleigh.

When they reached the house, which now seemed much larger and more majestic, the heady aroma of warm cinnamon carried them up each of the nineteen flagstone steps. The double front doors, paned with random bits of dark, stained glass, were held open by pewter sculptures of bees.

"Hello?" Kayleigh called in through the doorway.

Nothing moved, but there was sound. Music, slightly muted, drifted from somewhere not far inside.

Kayleigh looked at Lincoln and he shrugged, stepped forward and knocked loudly on the left door. "Mr. Tompkins?" he asked, then repeated his query more loudly.

No answer.

Cautiously, they entered.

The entryway opened onto both a living area to the left and a waiting room on the right, the walls of which were lined with shelf after shelf of books. As they moved silently into the living room, following the rise and fall of strings and oboes, Lincoln glanced at the spines of a few books in passing: *Provincial Beekeeping. Apiary Artisan. Backyard Beekeeper.*

"Lincoln, look!" Kayleigh whispered.

He followed her into the next room and the music came fully to life.

Expecting an ancient Victrola, or even a phonograph, they were surprised to discover a transparent crystal sitting upon a small, oval table. It was about a foot tall and constructed of pentagons. Kayleigh knew the name of this solid from Mr. Tegeyo's math class in a world left behind: a dodecahedron. The music, a relaxing yet intricate classical piece, seemed not to come from this crystal, but instead from an invisible sphere around it. Lincoln reached out and gently touched one of the twelve pentagonal surfaces. It was smooth and cool, but as his index finger caressed it, an array of multi-hued lights went off inside. The silent firework display lit the small room for only a second and the music changed. Mostly cellos and basses, this piece lent a dark and brooding quality to the house.

"Hello?"

Kayleigh and Lincoln jumped and spun around.

"Oh, sorry!" said the young man standing in the doorway. "I heard you come in, but didn't want to wake my father by calling back."

He took a step forward and offered his hand.

"I'm Joseph," he said.

Shaking his hand, Lincoln apologized. "Sorry. I'm Lincoln and this is Kayleigh. We're friends of Mona Tarok."

"How is she?" Joseph asked, leading them back into the living room.

"She's fine," Kayleigh said, noticing his concern. "She actually sent us here on an errand. We're hoping you can help us."

Joseph beamed. "Of course! That is, if it's something I can do. My Dad's a bit under the weather right now. He hates leaving me his chores, but I insisted he go to sleep early."

They started by telling him about the new "hostel".

"The one they're going to build on Mount Aikona?" he asked.

They nodded and explained that Mona was going to be meeting with Mayor Stitch about it tomorrow.

"My father is supposed to be at that same meeting! The business we'd make selling our honey at the hostel would more than double our profits."

Joseph excused himself and returned with a tray and three small mugs of hot tea.

"Sweetened with our honey, of course," he said, handing out the earthenware mugs, "but we grow the tea leaves, too."

Though neither of them were fans of hot tea, they sipped appreciatively at the surprisingly delicious drink.

"I think things over here just taste better," Lincoln said, smiling at Kayleigh.

Joseph's eyes narrowed at the comment. He motioned to a large, purple and black pinch pot on the table before them. Inside it were a collection of small, brown lumps wrapped in twisted squares of waxed paper.

Kayleigh took one and spun the paper open. She looked at their host questioningly.

"Go ahead," he said, and offered one to Lincoln. "I know they don't look like much."

Lincoln ate it quickly, then smiled and helped himself to another. Kayleigh finished the bit of chewy candy and said, "I can taste the honey, but there's something else, isn't there?"

Smiling himself, Joseph said, "It's not something we added, exactly, but rather how our bees make honey. They pollinate across the Trokamano Orchard and their nectar is a byproduct of rapture figs."

Lincoln stopped chewing midway through his third piece.

Their new friend laughed, "Don't worry. The honey has no trace of the rye creach toxins in the actual fruit."

Lincoln swallowed, but did not take another piece.

"So," Joseph began, "you mentioned the hostel?"

"Well," Kayleigh explained, "Mona said we might be able to borrow some of your father's old equipment."

He immediately knew where she was going. "I've been trying to get him to trade off those old tandem saws for years. I could never see how they'd ever be useful again. Now he's sure to say 'I told you so'."

"Would we be able to take them back with us tonight?" Lincoln asked.

Joseph rose and collected their mugs. "Not unless you came with a cart. We have about twelve of them and they're pretty heavy. Rusty, too."

Noticing the questioning look that passed between them, Joseph stopped and thought on it.

"You know," he said with a pause, "I'll be taking my father to that get-together tomorrow morning and we'll be passing right by the orchard. We could drive up and drop off those saws. We could even take Mona with us if she doesn't already have a ride."

Kayleigh brightened. "That sounds great, as long as it's okay with your father."

Joseph smiled again. "Dad loves a bit of company. Besides, he and M. Tarok will probably spend the entire ride talking shop and dreaming up new recipes for candies or preserves."

Noticing the failing light through the large living room window, Lincoln said, "We should probably head back. Rylyn…" he glanced at Kayleigh.

Startled by how much time had gone by, she rose.

Joseph followed them to the entryway.

About three steps before they reached the front door, Lincoln stopped. Kayleigh nearly fell into him, then steadied herself on his right arm. "What?" she asked.

Lincoln couldn't find the words at first, but she followed his gaze to a small, framed picture on the wall to their left. The photo, quite old, showed three young girls sitting together on a bench. Behind them was a wooden wall similar to that of the BTEL train stations. They wore spring dresses and held their clasped hands in their laps. It was the look in their eyes, however, that made Lincoln stop so quickly.

"Is that them?" Kayleigh asked. She turned to Joseph and at once noticed the uneasy expression on his face.

"Mona told us all about them," Kayleigh said. "We were actually hoping to meet them while we were here, but she said they had died."

"Well..." Joseph stammered, "They were quite old. Um, why exactly did you want to meet them?"

Lincoln tore his gaze from the photograph and noticed a definite change in their new friend's voice. "We had... business with them," Lincoln said, then (figuring this sounded too ominous) added, "More of a message. And a gift."

"Joseph?" a voice called from deep within the house.

Turning, Joseph stepped back into the living room. "Excuse me for not walking you out. My father... I'll see you tomorrow morning, okay?"

Without further comment, he left. Kayleigh and Lincoln took one final glance at the picture of the Corci sisters before leaving the house and making their way back to Mona.

7. Gathering

By the time they returned, Mona and Rylyn had just finished setting the wide kitchen table for dinner. Lincoln and Kayleigh, again, had immediate flashbacks to their first meeting with Mona at The Oak Hotel.

Rylyn, who was normally so careful with the few words she spoke, went on about the remainder of her afternoon with Godfray. With a slight blush, she talked excitedly about his family—on his mother's side, it was all Trader, but his great-grandfather founded a tiny fishing village on the northern Eastern Sea coast called Ceca Hebona. This is where most of his family still lived. Kayleigh offered Lincoln a smile, remembering the night they'd hidden under a small rescue boat when they'd first visited Ceca Hebona.

As Rylyn went on about how Godfray had been enlisted to work with the group of carpenters constructing the new hostel, Mona moved about with a look of trepidation. She called Kayleigh with her to retrieve a jar of preserves from the basement. When Mona had taken a random jar from a nearby shelf, she turned and said, "I have a really bad feeling about whatever you and Lincoln are going to be telling us."

Kayleigh sighed, then said, "No one is going to get hurt."

"Good," Mona said, "Because I've led a full life. Rylyn, however, is still a child, much like you. I can't imagine putting her in any trouble."

"If things go the way they're supposed to," Kayleigh said, helping Mona back up the stairs, "Rylyn might soon be the safest person in Burnam Tau'roh."

Dinner was, without exception, delicious. Rylyn continued on happily about Godfray while Mona looked on with veiled distress. By the time the dinner dishes were taken away and bowls of honeyed preserves and cream were served, Rylyn shyly excused herself for monopolizing the conversation.

"No need to apologize, dear," Mona said and squeezed the girl's hand gently.

Kayleigh leaned forward and scooped a bit of caramelized fruit onto her long, silver spoon and said, "Ben Tompkins and his son are stopping by tomorrow morning with the tandem saws."

Both Mona and Rylyn looked up at her.

"Joseph says you can ride along with them to the meeting if you want," Lincoln added.

Rylyn glanced at Mona, causing the old woman to let out a long-held breath. "I've already told Rylyn everything you've told me. There's nothing she doesn't know about what's happening so far."

"Good," Kayleigh said, relieved. "That will make this a little easier, I suppose."

Mona rose, walked to a shelf and returned with a thick candle on a dull, silver plate. She set it on the table between them. Rylyn moved quickly to the stove and returned with a thin stick. With the tiny flame burning at the tip, she lit the candle and extinguished the stick on the plate.

Kayleigh looked at Lincoln, then began, "In the time Lincoln and I come from, which to the both of you is the future, we know a different Mona Tarok. She looks just like you, Mona, but she is actually a collection of many different people. At some point in your life, you will pass on what is called your *sáwol,* or spirit, into a host that will assume your likeness. You will not die, but live on as the protector of the de'Malange. The *sáwol* of the oaks are on some great journey we're apparently helping with, but you are supposed to remain here to protect their bodies."

"And by *bodies,*" Mona said, "You mean their wood? The Oak Hotel?"

"Yes," Lincoln put in. "There is some quality to the wood, as well as the place where the trees once stood, that allows us to use Pandiments, which are kind of like spells that can change or create things."

"And," Kayleigh interrupted, taking Lincoln's hand. "We were given a new Pandiment for you, Mona. And for Rylyn."

Standing slowly, Rylyn asked, "Am I to be the person whom Mona will pass herself into?"

There was the longest, most perfect stretch of silence in the farmhouse kitchen.

"Yes," Kayleigh finally breathed. "It's called The Pandiment of the Oak Matron. Don't ask me what will happen, but Ka Tolerates told me it was created with great care and love and will protect you, both of you, as you take on this role."

Mona's worry seemed to lessen. She was now beside Rylyn with an arm around the girl.

Lincoln remembered something. "Rylyn, you don't have to do this. In order for the Pandiment to work, you have to agree."

Rylyn gave Mona a hug, then sat down and faced her new friends. "I'm in," she said and looked back at Mona, "You've taken me in and cared for me. This is the least I can do."

"What will happen to each of us? Our memories?" Mona asked, still standing.

"We don't know," Kayleigh admitted.

Collecting the empty dessert bowls, Mona asked, offhandedly, "When is this supposed to occur?"

"After all the trees have been delivered to the top of Mount Aikona," Lincoln said. "Once the actual construction has begun. We'll be gone, or at least I think we will. You two will go to the hotel alone and, Rylyn, you will have to read the Pandiment aloud."

Daylight had fled and night was upon them. With more to think about than speak of, Mona and Rylyn went off to bed.

"How did we do?" Lincoln asked, tracing the wooden veins and knots on the table with his index finger.

"Okay, I guess. I don't know. This whole thing is crazy."

Nodding, Lincoln said, "Yes it is. All of it."

They awoke to the dissonant, though not unpleasant sound of bells. Kayleigh ran into the side room where Lincoln slept and shook him awake. "Quick! They're here!"

Outside, they greeted Joseph and Ben and worked quickly to unload the burden of saws. Moving like ghosts in the pre-dawn light, Ben introduced himself to Kayleigh and Lincoln and offered a quick history of the equipment.

"I should have traded these off years ago, but they're all I have left of the old days. These were my great-grandfather's and he wagered everything he owned on a hand of Scarlet Daring to purchase them. What you have here are twelve crosscut M-tooths. They're the best felling saws around, even now. Unfortunately, I don't have a single bucking saw. You'd use them once your trees are on the ground, but these old timers will work in a pinch. I also threw in those crates of felling, splitting and broad axes. And a few hatchets. You never know when they might come in handy."

Kayleigh surveyed the wide collection of tools. "This is amazing, Mr. Tompkins! I can't believe how new it all looks!"

"Well," the older man said, looking down briefly at the ground beneath him. "I woke up early, so I had some time to clean 'em up a bit."

Lincoln moved forward and marveled at the assortment. The handles on each tool were well worn and smooth as river stone. The original designs that had been carved into them were barely visible, though Lincoln thought he recognized different types of leaves: poplar, maple, elm and small bunches of tiny pinecone and needle.

It was agreed that Rylyn would accompany both Mona and Ben to the meeting at Gate House and return in the late afternoon. It wasn't until they had left (the soft sound of clopping hooves fading down the orchard's main entrance) that Kayleigh and Lincoln realized Joseph had stayed behind.

"Why aren't—" Lincoln began, but was interrupted with a smile.

"It's okay," their new friend said, moving toward them with a small satchel. "My father and I worked it out." He moved to the porch and sat down with the worn bag in his lap.

"Worked what out?" Kayleigh asked.

"I should have told you before you left yesterday, but I had to be sure."

Kayleigh and Lincoln just stood there, staring into his wide and conspiratorial eyes.

"Okay," he began again, "The Corci sisters aren't dead."

"What?" Kayleigh breathed. They moved to the porch steps and sat down.

"Up until a month ago, they were still taking visitors, though no more than a dozen or so per day. Traders would bring in off-world groups just to meet them, but it was just too much. Some of us decided to help. We hid them away so they could live the remainder of their lives in peace. Seven families share this secret and each do their part to help take care of them. This here," he said, patting his bag, "Is what my father and I are able to do."

He found the drawstring and pulled it open. Lincoln leaned over. Inside were hundreds of pieces of the dark candy they'd sampled yesterday afternoon.

"It's a small thing, I guess, giving them candy. But they do love it. They're so lonely out there. Oh, and I brought these…"

He reached into his pocket and withdrew three small tickets, two of which he offered to them.

"You're going to take us to them, aren't you?" Kayleigh asked, smiling.

"If we leave right now, we should make the ticket station for the next train."

Kayleigh ran inside, made them each a cheese sandwich with some dark, spicy orange cheese she found, pushed it into Lincoln's pack and they were off. Just before they reached Ticket Station IX, Joseph turned and asked, "Could you guys do me a favor and just call me Joe?"

"You don't like Joseph?" Lincoln asked, understanding the sensitivity with names. He'd dealt with his share of kids teasing him over his name.

"It's not that. It's just... well, I don't have many friends, working with my father all the time. I've always had this picture in my mind of going out on some sort of adventure and no one would know me as Joseph the beekeeper. I'd just be *Joe*. I guess that sounds strange..."

"Actually, it doesn't," Kayleigh said, sidling up beside him. Lincoln came up on his left. "We've been on a pretty crazy adventure and we've met a lot of strange, scary and wonderful people along the way. You are now officially a part of our quest."

"Really?" he asked, and immediately seemed years younger.

"Absolutely, Joe," Lincoln added, offering a friendly punch on the arm.

They reached Ticket Station IX about a minute before the train arrived. The Ticketmaster, a sweet old woman who answered to the name Sassy, knew Joe and hinted at coming over to visit his father sometime next week. She had green eyes that simply glowed in the morning light. Kayleigh thought her a stark contrast to Clyde Manrope, the creepy Ticketmaster they'd met when they first arrived. Of course, it had been Stitch in disguise. At this thought, she found herself glancing back and forth as the train hissed to a full stop.

Lincoln couldn't help but smile.

"It's our train," he said to Kayleigh. "BTEL #3."

"It looks brand new," she said as they stepped up to the first car behind the engine.

Joe looked confused. "It is new, but I didn't think they were going to put her on the line for another week or two. I wonder what's going on?"

This question was answered a second later as the door hushed open and Truman Stitch stood smiling at the entrance. Joe cocked an eyebrow at the sudden appearance of the new Mayor. Kayleigh and Lincoln, however, did their best not to let their terror show.

"Ah," the Mayor spoke in his deep, resonant voice. "It appears that we have our first passengers."

From within the cab, a familiar female voice intoned, "If we are to keep our current schedule, they will need to board within the next forty-five point three seconds."

Smiling, though not quite smiling, Stitch called out, "Wonderful! Well, children, let's not keep our train waiting."

8. The Sisters

ithout knowing quite what was happening or how they had so quickly been pulled into the situation, Lincoln and Kayleigh were sitting across from the one person they most wanted to avoid. To balance out their nervousness, Stitch was both calm and filled with obvious joy. He rambled on about BTEL #3 and how this particular train was so special.

"...spared no expense," he continued, "It looks like the others, but special materials were used during construction. Ship? Oh, pardon me... Train?" he asked aloud. "What was the high stress metal used in your frame and hull?"

"It will one day be known as duraFLEX-9, a carbon and aluminum nanocomposite, M. Stitch," the train spoke smoothly.

The new Mayor smiled. "It will no doubt outlast the others. Yes... I have big plans for this little train."

They let Stitch do most of the talking, afraid that in making polite conversation they would somehow give themselves away. This came to an end, however, when he leaned forward and looked at each of them in turn.

"Well," he said, looking at Joe, "I'm going to wager a wild guess that you're Ben Tompkins's boy."

Joe, who had no real reason to be alarmed, smiled slightly and said, "That's correct, Sir. My father is with M. Tarok at Gate House as we speak."

"Splendid!" Truman boomed and clapped Joe on the knee. "Wonderful! I am on my way there as well." He turned his attention to Kayleigh and Lincoln and narrowed his eyes, "You two, now... have we met before?"

Lincoln froze. They couldn't tell him their real names, but they couldn't lie. Lincoln wasn't sure Joe would understand so quickly what they were doing. Kayleigh jumped in before he could think any further on it.

"My name is Kayleigh and this is Lincoln," she said. Lincoln supposed she sounded calm, but he did notice her rubbing her thumb and index finger nervously together against her knee.

Kayleigh wondered whether or not she should mention Mona, but Joe saved the moment by explaining how they were helping him take care of an errand for his father.

"How responsible of you," Stitch smiled. "How far will you be taking my wonderful BTEL #3 this morning?"

Joe started to speak, then bit his lip. He looked toward Lincoln, but Lincoln had nothing to save them.

"We're on our way to the Painted Lighthouse," Kayleigh blurted out, filling the odd silence between them.

"The Painted… *Lighthouse*?" Stitch asked, eyes narrowing.

The silence that followed was much more uncomfortable this time.

Stitch's voice was slow and muddy, as if he'd just waken from a dream, "I didn't know we had a—"

The train shook slightly, then began to break.

"M. Stitch, we will be stopping at Gate House in approximately 45 seconds."

Stitch reached beside his seat and pulled a small, leather satchel onto his lap. Opening it and checking its contents, he glanced nervously over to the strangers. Kayleigh managed a weak, equally troubled smile. Lincoln could barely swallow and felt a sick, solid knot twist just below his ribcage.

The train slowed to a stop. A glance outside the window allowed a view both Kayleigh and Lincoln had not seen before in Burnam Tau'roh. Instead of wilderness and woodland, there were crushed-stone paths and roads leading to all manner of small buildings. The largest was a pentagonal, two-story structure surrounded by flowering purple bushes. A beautifully carved wooden sign sat before it: Gate House.

Stitch rose and walked quickly to the door. As it hushed open, he turned back. "I look forward to speaking with your father," he said amiably, nodding at Joe. He said nothing more before stepping out of the car. BTEL #3 waited another ten seconds, then closed its door and continued southward down the line. Through the window, they watched as he crossed the tracks and moved toward a young woman they knew to be Sheenie Tosh.

"So, that was Truman Stitch," Joe said, breaking the five minutes of silence that followed the Mayor's departure.

Lincoln stared at Kayleigh's right hand. Her fingers still rubbed anxiously against her knee. She finally glanced up and nodded at Joe, then turned and stared hard at Lincoln.

"I know," she said, "You don't have to say it."

Lincoln felt a dull pang of guilt. He'd almost stated the obvious, that the Painted Lighthouse had not yet been built. He turned to Joe and asked, "Why didn't you tell him about the Corci sisters?"

Joe looked down at his shoes, then glanced back up at them. "Well, as I've said it's a secret."

"But there's more to it than that, right?" Kayleigh asked.

Joe let out a breath of air. "Yes, but you two have to swear not to mention this to anyone, okay? My dad would lose it if he knew I was telling you this."

"We have something to share with you, too, when you're done. Something we probably shouldn't tell either, so go ahead."

"Fine," Joe began. "I'm not sure how long ago this happened, but it couldn't have been too long after Truman Stitch first arrived. From what I heard, the first thing he did when we arrived was track down the Corcis. They are the sweetest ladies you'll ever meet, but Truman must have said or done something because after that visit, they refused to talk to anyone. Nova Reckór, our old mayor, has been taking care of them for many years and when she heard what happened with Stitch, she withdrew early from her position and disappeared with the Corcis. My father thinks that's why Truman did whatever he did… to get M. Reckór out of her position so quickly."

"This all sounds just like the Truman Stitch we know and *don't* love," Lincoln said.

"What were you going to say?" Joe asked Kayleigh.

She took a deep breath and looked at Lincoln. His look said, simply, *Go ahead, we've got nothing to lose.*

"It's a lot to take in," Kayleigh began, "But here it goes…"

As far as explaining their insane adventure, Lincoln thought she did a pretty good job condensing it into the space of about fifteen minutes. As the train began slowing to their stop, Kayleigh wrapped it up with an explanation of their familiarity with the voice on the train.

"So you think this is the same train you rode in your future?" Joe asked.

"Pretty sure," Kayleigh said.

Joe shook his head, smiling, "You know what? I believe you. I don't know why, but I believe all of it. You know what's crazy, though? Not that you've traveled back in time to be here, but that everything is almost magically falling into place for you. It's amazing how chance meetings with people can change things."

Lincoln found that he could not return the smile. "I have a feeling our tree friends have influenced things more than we thought. I don't think *chance* means the same thing to them."

The train pulled to a complete stop.

"I'm afraid I must point out," the smooth, female voice of the train spoke suddenly, "That the nearby settlement to the west of our current location may not be safe."

"We're not going to Shora Cessyu," Joe said, matter-of-factly. "We're actually heading east toward the Sughi. We're... going to hike our way overland."

Without further comment, the door slid open and the three friends disembarked.

"Did it know you were lying?" Lincoln asked as they began down a path paved with mulched wood.

"I don't know," Joe said, kicking at a piece of bark sticking up from the ground. "I've never lied to a talking train before."

"There's nothing we can do about it now anyway," Kayleigh added. "Now that we've officially bumped into Stitch, I want to get things done as quickly as... *no way!*"

"What?" Lincoln asked. She turned to him with a spooked look in her eyes.

"Do you remember when we got off BTEL #3 for the first time and I stayed behind for a second?"

Lincoln nodded, barely recalling Kayleigh hesitating before joining him.

"The train said something to me, but it didn't make any sense."

"What did it say?" Joe asked, intrigued.

"It said, 'I never forget a face'. That explains how Stitch knew so much about what we were doing."

"And how he got to Shipmaster Creek so quickly."

"*And,*" Kayleigh added, "How he knew we were headed to Te'hæra Thorn."

"I think I'll stick with BTEL #1 and #2 from now on," Joe said, which lightened the mood a bit. Kayleigh actually smiled, though tried without success to rid her mind of the train's eerie voice.

On their first visit to Shora Cessyu, Kayleigh and Lincoln weren't sure what they were getting into. They didn't expect a town of small, abandoned houses inhabited by ghostly spirits.

They didn't expect a working movie theater. In no way did they expect to meet up with an impersonated Shipmaster Creek.

This time, expecting a sinister landscape, they were surprised to discover the small houses bright and cheerful, each one painted light and airy pastel colors. The miniature front lawns were well tended and host to carefully manicured topiary. Sitting at porches or talking over fences were the smallest people they had ever seen. They weren't dwarfish in nature or build. They were human, just on a smaller scale.

"You were holding my hand the last time we walked through here," Kayleigh said to Lincoln, smiling.

In awe of what he was seeing, Lincoln still heard the amusement in her voice and quickly slid his hand into hers.

"Don't let go," she said, her serious words hidden behind the smile.

"Never," he said.

Joe, who had until then not guessed how close these two marvelous strangers might be, smiled to himself, slightly envious not only of this intimacy, but the impossible nature of the quest they were on.

They continued on down the main road and waved to those who called out simple greetings. The thick toll of bells filled the air and they looked down the street to the Cinema. Except, now, it wasn't the Cinema. The gaudy marquee lights and framed movie posters were gone, or had (in fact) not yet been added. The building was beautiful in its current, undisturbed state. Stained glass windows filled each portal like sleepy, knowing eyes.

"So it *was* a church," Kayleigh said.

"It is much more than simply a church," a voice stated from behind them. They turned.

Joe smiled and moved quickly to offer a hug. "Kayleigh. Lincoln. This is Nova Reckór."

As they exchanged greetings, Kayleigh was caught by the woman's stare. She watched Kayleigh as if they had met before.

"I—" Kayleigh began.

"I can explain," Nova said, smiling, her intense look replaced by pure kindness. "Come."

Following her back the way they had come, the previous mayor of Burnam Tau'roh took Kayleigh's arm into her own. "I knew this day would come to pass. The old girls spoke of it so long ago, though. Are you truly Kell-Korai? Queen of the Oaks?"

Not enjoying the title or being placed into a position she had not earned, Kayleigh immediately frowned.

"I mean no disrespect," Nova said at once, reading Kayleigh's face. "I use these names only to identify, as they were given to me years ago in my own reading."

"A reading by the Corci sisters," Joe explained.

"That is correct," Nova smiled, leading them through a miniature white, picket gate and up a cobblestone path to the porch of one of the houses. "I have known the old dears for a long time, but I'll always remember the reading I received when I first met them."

Nova stopped at the front door, put her hand to the small, brass knob and turned to look first at Kayleigh, then Lincoln.

"And now," she said, "it appears that what they told me is about to come true."

The interior of the small house was dim. There were no walls, or perhaps there had once been walls, but they now found themselves in a single room. Few furnishings adorned this painfully symmetrical space and Lincoln at once singled out a small, grandfather-style clock. The pendulum moved, though far too slowly to actually record the true passing of time. According to the face of the clock (which consisted of six hands pointing to a seemingly unrelated circle of numbers)

the "time" was 42, 23, 16, 15, 8, 4. Whatever that meant, Lincoln thought.

Kayleigh took no notice of the clock. She, instead, watched Nova pad quietly across the short distance to three thickly padded chairs. The women occupying the seats were far older than Kayleigh had imagined they would be. They may not have been identical triplets at birth, but now there was no telling them apart.

"Good afternoon," Nova said, kneeling before them. "I've brought you some visitors."

At once, the women turned in the direction of Nova's voice and Lincoln remembered that the Corci sisters were blind. They said nothing to Nova's greeting, but smiled beatifically.

Nova moved toward the back of the room and stood beside Joe as Kayleigh and Lincoln moved toward the seated women. Their three heads seemed to turn in unison toward the sound of approaching feet. When Kayleigh stood before them, she knelt, then motioned to Lincoln to do the same.

"We have come a great distance to see you," Kayleigh began, then stopped, her throat dry.

"We thought we were going to meet three little girls," Lincoln said without thinking, filling the silence.

The sisters smiled, then introduced themselves in the order in which they sat: Mynah, Hymna and Ahnmy.

"The main reason for our visit is to keep a promise," Kayleigh said.

"Yes," Mynah spoke, her voice as thin as sun-bleached rice paper. "You promised yourself an enchantment that would bring you here."

Lincoln shrugged off his worn backpack and pulled it open. After a second or two of digging, he recovered a bruised box of PopTop Taffy. Tearing off the top, he carefully eased the box into Mynah Corci's hands.

She pulled out a small piece of salt-water taffy and pulled at each end of the wrapper. Smiling, she placed the pink section of taffy carefully into her mouth. She did not appear to chew on it, but instead savored the flavor as it melted away on her tongue. Passing the box down to her sisters, Hymna and Ahnmy also took a piece and their smiles matched that of Hymna.

"What is it that you ask of us, young man?" Hymna queried, leaning slightly forward in her chair.

"Well... we came to ask for the Pandiment of Time, the spell you spoke of, but I guess we already have it." Lincoln took the scrap of paper from his pack and held it out before them.

"Lincoln," Kayleigh nudged him. "They can't see it."

"Oh," he said, face reddening.

"It appears," Ahnmy said softly, "That you will need to hide this important item safely for its return trip forward. Is there a place you can put it where it will remain untouched?"

"Oh," Nova said, reaching down to a stack of books behind the open front door. "What about here? These are journals of my time as mayor in Burnam Tau'roh. By the decree of our province, no record book shall ever be destroyed, but saved for future generations."

Kayleigh took one of the books from her, opened to a random page and Lincoln dropped the wrinkled piece of rapture fig wrapper between the pages. Closing the book, she handed it back to Nova, who returned it to the stack.

"What's done, is done," Mynah said, her smile fading. "Though I fear there is more at work here."

"We knew that Truman Stitch would arrive, but not the amount of damage he would bring," Hymna added.

A thought passed through Kayleigh's mind and she spoke impulsively. "Something terrible is going to happen to this town," she began. "When we first visited here, in your future, the houses were filled with spirits or ghosts. It was a horrible feeling walking down the street. And the church, or whatever it is, was a movie theater."

"The man who works there, Shipmaster Creek, is the person who gave us your taffy," Lincoln said.

101

The expressions on their faces did not change, but it was Ahnmy who spoke:

"So you have brought your own predictions, but please speak no more of the future. As your special friend as no doubt already told you, the past, present and future are delicate things and are not to be altered without the greatest of care."

Friend? Kayleigh thought. Did they know of the de'Malange? Before she could ask the question, Mynah's smile returned and she patted her lap: "Here, my children."

Both Kayleigh and Lincoln leaned forward and placed their open palms into the old woman's hands.

9. Preparations

For a long moment, Mynah said nothing. Her cool, dry fingers moved effortlessly over both Kayleigh and Lincoln's open hands. Her face grew somber as nearly a full minute passed.

To Kayleigh, she said softly, "Your Grandmother will soon be revealed to you."

To Lincoln, she said, "Can't trust him."

103

With conflicting emotions in their hearts, they moved to Hymna. The room was impossibly quiet and although they knew they were being watched, Kayleigh and Lincoln felt as if they were entombed twenty feet underground. There were no open windows, but a stale breeze brushed past them.

To Kayleigh, Hymna whispered, "The Queen's responsibility is for the first oak as well as the last." When she was done tracing the avenues of Lincoln's palm, she frowned and said, "What you seek is wrapped deeply in time."

The false grandfather clock behind them chimed a lonely tune and doled out a cryptic count of nine.

They moved with trepidation toward Ahnmy. Her fingers moved more slowly than her sisters. She touched certain areas of Kayleigh's hand over and over again and, drawing circles around the tips of her fingers. After careful consideration, she licked her lips and said, "Kayleigh must die."

Kayleigh pulled back in shock. Lincoln did the same, but Ahnmy took his wrist with impossible strength. She needed only to pass her open palm across his to complete the final reading. She spoke clearly, but sadly. "You must learn how to say goodbye."

When Ahnmy finally let go of his hand, Kayleigh took it and they raced outside of the miniature house.

"No!" Lincoln hissed. "No way. That is not going to happen."

His face was flushed with anger and fear, but Kayleigh put her hands on his arms to steady him and said, simply, "Calm down."

"Calm down? Are you crazy?" he asked.

"Probably," she said, although her voice was a bit shaky. "We can't take everything they said literally. There might be other meanings to what they told us."

Lincoln refused to listen, shaking his head. "*Kayleigh must die* doesn't leave much room for alternate meanings."

She let go as Lincoln began to pace aimlessly up and down the empty street. Though her palm reading was far from happy, seeing Lincoln like this really bothered her. Catching up with him, she said, "Maybe it just means that one day when I'm, like, a hundred years old I'll be walking down the street and an old tree will fall on me."

Lincoln looked up at her, but couldn't fully return the smile she offered.

"With your luck, it'll probably be an oak tree," he murmured.

They heard a door open and close. Joe walked quickly over to them.

"They're about to fall asleep," he told them. "I guess the readings tired them out. Nova is looking after them."

"Too bad they didn't get a chance to read your palm," Lincoln said wryly.

"They did," Joe said.

"Really?" Kayleigh asked.

"Yeah. I never asked them, even before, but when you guys left, they called me over."

"What did they say," Kayleigh asked after a brief moment of silence.

Joe shook his head. "Well… it didn't make much sense. Mynah said I should remember to feed Gepeto, Hymna said to watch out for Sidhera and Ahnmy said something about Grendesh. It's crazy. I haven't the slightest idea what any of that means."

Kayleigh turned to Lincoln.

"Ha!" she said. "It's like putting a coin in that creepy fortune teller machine at the Autumn Harbor Carnival. Or shaking a Magic 8 Ball. *Outlook Hazy. Ask Again Later.* Lincoln, it could mean anything."

They turned to Joe, whose face registered even more confusion.

Lincoln finally laughed and Kayleigh joined in. Joe shook his head and smiled, turning to Nova Rekor, who had just exited the house.

"They're asleep, the poor dears. I, um… don't know quite what to say about what happened in there."

In the distance, the sound of a train whistle sliced through the silence.

Nova straightened. "I'll be needed at Gate House toward the end of the meeting. I'm supposed to officially turn over my post as Mayor to M. Stitch. We might as well walk together to the train."

They left Shora Cessyu and the sleeping Corci sisters. Kayleigh felt a heavy weight upon her soul and Lincoln felt helpless and sick. Joe felt as if he had just stepped through a thick cloud of déjà-vu. Still, they managed to smile a bit and bid their friend Nova farewell before catching (thankfully) BTEL #1 back to Trokamano Orchards.

They were hoping Joe would stay for dinner, but he explained that whenever the Apiary was left alone for such a stretch there was always work to catch up on. They said their farewells when Ben, Mona and Rylyn returned mid-afternoon.

Ben was in a wonderful mood, going on about how great business would be over the next few seasons due to Mayor Stitch's new plan. Both Mona and Rylyn were nearly silent and visibly exhausted. After seeing Ben and Joe off, Mona led everyone inside and they gathered around the large kitchen table. Rylyn filled four large, wooden mugs with icy water lightly sweetened with nectar and cinnamon.

For the first few minutes, no one said a thing.

"Oh, dear," Mona finally said. "This is truly horrible."

"What happened?" Kayleigh asked.

"Truman is going to ruin everything. He tried to hide his intentions, but I could see through everything. He promised everyone a new and better Burnam Tau'roh. He promised more jobs. More income from all the tourists that will be coming through. He announced my position at the Oak Hotel."

"Wait," Lincoln said. "He actually called it the Oak Hotel?"

"Um, that was my fault," Rylyn said. "I couldn't get the name you used for it out of my head. M. Stitch overheard me tell Ben how strange it will be to see the Oak Hotel there on the top of Mount Aikona."

"He is going to bleed our land dry," Mona said bitterly. "I know that I'm aware of more than most here because of what you two have told me, but I can actually see it all beginning to happen already. I don't like it one bit."

Kayleigh and Lincoln took deep breaths and spoke of their adventure to Shora Cessyu. Kayleigh thought it strange how easy it was to retell the odd prophecies of three sisters, almost as if it had happened to a different Kayleigh and Lincoln. Both Mona and Rylyn didn't seem as upset as she thought they'd be, or maybe it was just Kayleigh's imagination.

There were no surprises concerning the Gate House meeting. They all knew what to expect and what was expected of them. Finally, Mona leaned forward and said, "Alright, my young friends. Since I am now what Stitch calls his Oak Matron—" she shuddered at this, "—my first duty is to contact our sources in Western Burnam Tau'roh and make ready for a very expensive shipment of lumber."

Another silence.

"This is the part I'm still a bit hazy on," Mona said. "How exactly are we supposed to get all of those magical trees cut down and transferred to Mount Aikona? I'd love to lend a hand, but—"

Kayleigh stretched and covered a yawn. "You and Rylyn are going to be busy enough on this side, Mona. Lincoln and I will take care of what happens on the other."

Kayleigh looked into Lincoln's eyes and said, "Ka Tolerates said she'd tell us everything else when we returned. So I guess we need to go back and get things started."

"At least wait until morning," Mona said, a haunted look in her eyes. "I have a feeling that getting this hotel built is going to take every last bit of our strength, both physical and mental. At least we have Nova, Ben and Joseph on our side. Ben will have a small crew pick up and deliver the equipment to Mount Aikona tomorrow at noon."

Rylyn said nothing, but nodded thoughtfully. Lincoln felt a pang of sorrow for the girl. He tried to think of something to say to ease her worry, but instead reached over and set his hand atop hers. Rylyn looked up at him, torn from her thoughts, but gave him the smile he was hoping for. Kayleigh caught the exchange and took Lincoln's free hand in her own.

"I don't know how," Kayleigh whispered, "but we're all going to get through this."

With the heel of her hand pressed to her right eye, Mona stood and turned away from the children. "Good, then. Very good. To sleep with all of us."

None could have ever guessed, especially Lincoln or Kayleigh, how many times they would think back on that final night's rest and long for the priceless hours of uninterrupted sleep.

About an hour before dawn, the eastern sky was impatient with muted, violet light. Lincoln sat on the front porch of the farmhouse, going through the items in his pack. There wasn't much left. The candy had been delivered to the sisters and all the popcorn had been eaten, though he did find a stale, flattened piece in the bottom corner. In a small pouch in the front were their treasures from the very beginning of the journey—the strange coin, the photograph and the tiny, black bottle.

"Here," Kayleigh said, exiting the house. She knelt down and deposited an armload of items. One by one, Lincoln tucked them into the backpack, conserving as much space as possible: three loaves of bread, three jars of rapture fig preserves, tightly wrapped bundles of spicy, dried meat, some cheese and an old canteen filled with water.

"I'll strap the canteen around my back since you have the bag," Kayleigh said, making sure the metal cap was screwed on tightly. "Sorry I lost mine when we fell from the lighthouse."

Lincoln smiled. "It wasn't your fault. The things that really mattered were in this one, anyway."

Mona and Rylyn walked them to the end of the driveway. As soon as Kayleigh turned to say goodbye, a sick feeling filled her stomach.

Mona tried to smile, but couldn't. Rylyn appeared as if she were using every bit of willpower not to cry.

"I have a bad feeling we won't be seeing each other again," Kayleigh said.

"I was thinking the same thing," Mona said softly as Kayleigh leaned in for a hug.

"It was nice meeting the real you," Lincoln said, joining in on the embrace. Rylyn stood off to the side, squeezing her eyes shut and doing her best to breathe.

When Mona broke away, she grew serious. "If you hear a train, move off into the trees. You don't want any more surprise visitors along the way."

Lincoln laughed nervously. "Only we would be so lucky meeting Stitch a third time."

Just as the sun spilled its first drops of morning onto the tree-covered hills, they left the orchard and headed northeast toward Mount Aikona.

10. Queen of the Oaks

kyCarOne shimmered like an Airstream trailer in the bright morning light, carrying its two passengers heavenward to the empty mountaintop. A cool and steady breeze followed them toward the eastern edge of the plateau.

"It's strange not seeing the lighthouse out there," Lincoln said as they moved across the featureless ground.

Kayleigh put a flattened hand to her eyes to shield the sun and nodded. "Otherwise, it looks pretty much the same. Is this where you planted that acorn?"

Lincoln glanced around, then pointed to a dark area of disturbed soil. "There," he said.

There was the premonition of a whisper just before the portal opened. They both heard the insistent voice of Ka Tolerates urging them onward. *Now*, it said without words. *The time has come.* Holding hands, they crossed over and broke into a run.

Quickly, my children!

Something was wrong and they both felt it. Kayleigh actually allowed a bit of anger to balance her sense of urgency. *The de'Malange can manipulate space and time and basically control our lives,* she fumed. *So how can they not foresee things that will go wrong?*

When they reached Ka Tolerates, they were stunned to find all of the Pilgrims standing in a semi-circle around the tree. Kayleigh imagined it must have been nearly every citizen of Kana Hove.

"What—?" Lincoln began, but was silenced by the hurried voice of the tree.

We have little time. Stitch in your world knows far more than he should. Something, impossibly, has changed. It might have been your placement in the earlier Burnam Tau'roh. Either way, he suspects something. The wood from our trees needs to be over there as quickly as possible. Construction must commence at once. The Pilgrims are here to assist you before they join us.

"I don't see my Grandfather," Kayleigh said.

He is already asleep. He will sleep as long as it takes for the Valley of Oaks to be cleaned.

Kayleigh started to speak, but held her words back, unsure of how to proceed.

Dear child, do not fear for us. The oaks are only our bodies. Before you begin taking us down, we will leave and watch over you. You will never be alone. We knew this day would come and we are ready. It is now time for you, Queen Kell-Korai, to answer your destiny.

Kayleigh looked at Lincoln and knew what he was thinking. They'd spent all this time seeing the oaks as spiritual, revered beings and now they had to brutally cut them all down. Everything about what they were doing made them both feel sick.

Lincoln, please remember that you are not here by accident. You stand beside the Queen and honor us. Your help in this great task is immeasurable. You still have the glass vial?

Lincoln nodded, feeling the weight of the pack on his back.

"Yes," he said weakly. "But where did it come from? Mona said that a sick man came to the hotel and—"

Its origins are, strangely, unknown to us. It is, however, vital to our journey. The nature of the glass will protect our sawol during the great journey.

Pearle Kho, the woman they had met on their previous trip, walked up to them from the group of people.

"We are ready to do what needs to be done," she said and knelt before Kayleigh. With this simple act, the entire assemblage dropped to one knee and placed crossed arms over their hearts.

There was only the empty sound of the wind through the high boughs of the oaks. Kayleigh knew now why everything felt so strange. The de'Malange had already left the oaks. The trees were only trees now… or were they?

Not so high above the hill behind them, in the direction of Kana Hove, they watched a familiar, ethereal ribbon of prismatic light float and spin in the air. They first spied this miracle the night they arrived in Burnam Tau'roh. This time, as well, they heard the distant, beautiful music of children… an impossible choir of angelic voices speaking an incomprehensible message of love and hope.

Lincoln's eyes filled with tears, though he could not explain why.

Kayleigh looked back into the face of Pearle Kho and bit down on her bottom lip. "Okay!" she said out loud, addressing the Pilgrims. "No one is looking forward to what must be done."

And just then, something changed. Kayleigh couldn't explain it to herself, but a feeling blanketed her, carrying specific knowledge that the oaks needed to be hewn and delivered in a specific order. Certain trees would frame the base of the Oak Hotel. Others would be used for siding. Still others would be set aside and fashioned into one of many doors. She understood that this would make their job more difficult, but it was vitally important that it be done in this manner. Those who would build the hotel would somehow know how to use this lumber, but first she had to organize it.

Kayleigh took a long, shuddering breath. This must be why I was chosen, she thought, then stared out into the mass of waiting faces. When she spoke, her voice was stronger. The gathering immediately stood at attention as if they knew they were in the presence of a true leader.

"We're going to have to work in teams, my friends. I don't know how long this will take, but we must not stop until this dreadful job is finished."

There were no cheers of assent or acknowledgement. Instead, they smiled and nodded, letting her know that they were hers to lead.

Turning, taking Lincoln's hand, she led them all back through the silent Valley of the Oaks.

They retrieved the large, unwieldy saws that belonged to Ben Tompkins and immediately set to work. The awful task of felling the oaks was immediately made worse by the pure difficulty of the act. The saws were, at best, dull. It took not two, but four or even six people to handle each rusty tool. The wooden handles, worn smooth, soon grew weak and cracked, sending uncounted splinters into every hand that worked them. After a few hours, with only a few trees down, Kayleigh reorganized the groups into rotations for work, rest and supplies. Most of the Pilgrims were not up to the grueling labor and tired quickly. "Supply" groups made trips back to Kana Hove to return with food, water and blankets for sleeping.

After a full day of work, they had only nineteen oaks to show for it. The great valley of trees stood around them, silent and imposing. For the first time in thousands of years, the

Symphony of Dusk did not fill the air with thoughtful sorrow as the sun set. Not once did Kayleigh voice her dreaded opinion, crying out that this was simply impossible. She couldn't imagine how they would do it, even working on it for a year. She and Lincoln spent most of their time together with their group, falling exhausted onto rough blankets on the damp, mossy ground when their shifts were over.

The portal opened by Ka Tolerates connecting Kana Hove to the Burnam Tau'roh of the past opened instantaneously whenever they were ready to transport the trees through. Along with the extra hatchets and other miscellaneous tools that Ben Tompkins had left for them was a stack of about twenty logging frocks. They were grey and had a silver-embroidered logo of branches sprouting from the letter 'T'. The teams transferring the wood wore them on the Burnam Tau'roh side just in case someone (Truman) was watching. Although days passed in the valley between deliveries, the portal always opened just after the previous shipment had been delivered. By the time they carried through their twentieth allotment of oaks, weeks after they had started, only a handful of hours had passed atop the silent Mount Aikona.

Late one afternoon, Pearle Kho came up to Kayleigh and Lincoln's group just after they returned through the portal. They were exhausted, covered with dirt and sap and more than

119

ready to put their hatchets away until the next delivery. Pearle held out a small device the size and shape of a ballpoint pen. "I meant to bring this to your attention a week ago, but I think someone came to the top of your mountain to see what was going on. This was found just outside the portal." Holding it up, she accidentally pressed a tiny button and a bright strobe of light blinded them all. Stumbling back and rubbing her eyes, she said, ashamed, "I should probably just put this back where I found it."

That evening, Kayleigh snapped awake and rocked Lincoln back and forth.

"It can't possibly be time to get up already," Lincoln murmered.

"It's not," she whispered, careful not to wake the others sleeping around them. "I just thought of something. Can you get that photo out of your bag?"

Lincoln rolled over and unzipped one of the many pockets. He sat up beside her and held out the picture. Leaning close to him, Kayleigh smiled. For a moment, Lincoln didn't make the connection, but soon his eyes grew wide.

"No way!" he hissed.

They had stared at this old photo many times, but only now did it make sense. It was taken, of course, on Tehaera Thorn, as evidenced by the two suns in the background. The identity of the loggers, however, was now clear. It was them! Their group! With this knowledge, both Kayleigh and Lincoln recognized themselves in the group as well.

"How come we didn't see ourselves before?" Lincoln asked.

"Just look at us," Kayleigh giggled. "We're a complete mess. Plus, we're wearing those old logging uniforms."

"So," Lincoln said, careful to keep his voice down. "That thing Nova flashed at us was probably some sort of camera."

"It must have been," Kayleigh replied, still staring at herself and Lincoln. "We've changed."

"Well, we're a bit older."

"True, but in other ways, too.

Kayleigh often wondered about her Grandfather, Emil. When he had spoken of this time in his life, he thought he'd only slept for one night when he woke to discover the oaks and his fellow Pilgrims gone. He had no idea how much time had truly passed. She wanted to go with a supply group to the silent city and see him. She wanted to lay her head against his, to somehow let him know that she now understood a bit more of what he must have gone through.

Ka Tolerates spoke seldom during this time, but when Kayleigh had nearly convinced herself to visit Emil, the last oak tree spoke clearly into her mind.

There is nothing to be gained by seeing him. Know that he is safe and well protected.

Kayleigh told Lincoln and he agreed. Emil did not know of their involvement, so it didn't make sense to risk changing things.

When it was their turn to rest, which most often involved disturbing dreams, they fell asleep back-to-back, sharing what little warmth their bodies created on the cold ground. When it was time to resume work, they usually found their fingers laced tightly together as if in fear of being torn apart. By the fifth week, Kayleigh no longer tried to mask her feelings and sobbed into Lincoln's shoulder before they rose to join their group: "I don't want to die. You have to save me. You can't let this happen. I never want to leave you. I need you."

Deep inside, Lincoln was falling apart, but for Kayleigh he kept up a false front of hope and strength. She put up a similar front for the others, but unburdened herself on him.

"We're just kids, right?" she asked one night before falling into a troubled sleep.

Lincoln grew so terribly angry and whispered, "Not any more. We stopped being kids when we fell onto the bottom of the other side of Mount Aikona." And when he knew that Kayleigh was asleep, his anger was punctuated by hot, salty tears. He turned to Kayleigh and took her hands into his. Gently, he caressed the bloody cracks and abraded skin, the dark, sap-hardened bumps of her knuckles. He grew even more angry and closed his eyes. We are not children. We are not children.

We were never children.

The impossible was finally accomplished.

Nearly seven weeks after they started, they had somehow managed to cut down and transfer every oak in the valley. Forty-nine days of physical and mental agony ended only in the misplaced guilt of what they had done.

When the suns rose on the morning that found the valley filled with only the flat discs of stumps, each Pilgrim came up to Kayleigh with one of the many basins they used for drinking water. They scooped up small amounts of the cool water and poured them carefully onto Kayleigh's hands. Of course, their hands were equally blistered and blood-caked, but this small act allowed the Pilgrims to communicate what words could not.

Lincoln stood beside her and his body felt numb. As each Pilgrim soothed Kayleigh's hands, they turned and disappeared back toward Ka Tolerates. Soon, they would all join the magical rainbow light that spun in the sky of Te'hæra Thorn.

Lincoln moved before Kayleigh and brought her hands up to his dry lips to gently kiss her palms. She attempted a smile, but failed. The full force of her emotions was let loose and tears flooded her eyes. Without a thought, Lincoln caught her before she could fall to the ground. He did not even think of following the Pilgrims. Exhausted himself, he somehow managed to carry her to the silky black rotation of the portal between worlds.

The voice of Ka Tolerates spoke to them one final time, though her voice was soft in their minds.

I love you both. Please rescue me.

When they arrived back on Mount Aikona, there was barely enough space to walk. The trees, stacked in pyramids of six or ten, covered the entire mountaintop. Lincoln took a few careful steps away from the portal and knelt with Kayleigh still in his arms.

"What are you doing?" she asked, yawning.

Lincoln reached down into the dark soil in which he had planted the acorn days (weeks) ago. His fingers found the brown-green orb and gently pulled it up. It had not slept in the rich earth long enough to sprout or send out its first, single root.

Tapping off the dirt, he slipped it into his pack where it rested against the dark, cool glass of the tiny bottle. Kayleigh's breath had slowed to a steady, even rhythm. This, he thought, was a good thing.

Standing, he carried her with the greatest care toward the waiting SkyCarOne.

Just before he reached the conveyance, there was a slight cracking sound and three solid *thunks!* Lincoln turned in time to see one of the trees from their last delivery complete a ten-foot roll and drop over the edge of the cliff.

He stood before SkyCarOne and waited for the distant splash before taking Kayleigh down.

When Kayleigh opened her eyes, she was staring up into what appeared to be the late afternoon sky. She was leaning back against Lincoln's shoulder and could hear the slow pulse of his breathing. In the distance, there was birdsong that echoed between the low trees.

They were in the center of a mossy meadow where red and yellow lichen grew on the exposed surfaces of rocks. Kayleigh just lay there and took one breath at a time. Her hands still throbbed, but she pulled her mind away from her body and watched the tops of the trees move lazily to and fro in the breeze.

"Are you ready to go back?" Lincoln asked.

Kayleigh jumped slightly at his voice, then rolled her head to see him. He looked, she supposed, as horrible as she did. There were dark patches beneath his tired, haunted eyes.

"Go back?" she asked and pulled up to kneel before him.

Lincoln looked behind her and she followed his gaze. A softball-sized circle had been dug out of the smooth layer of moss. In its place was rich, loamy earth.

"Sometimes," Lincoln rasped, then swallowed. "When things like this happen, I feel like we're being protected."

"What things?" Kayleigh asked. She tried to stand, but felt so dizzy she had to sit back down.

"It's like everything we're doing is circular," Lincoln began. "And we just finished drawing one really big circle."

Kayleigh was lost and frustrated for not knowing what he was talking about. He must have seen this in her expression, for he smiled, leaned forward and helped her to her feet. She still felt a bit swimmy, but with his help remained upright.

Lincoln spoke aloud:

"O deliver me!
Twilight deep within the wood
Across the great void.

Many directions
In a dark and frozen sea
Are forever yours."

The portal that opened was not as powerful as the one Ka Tolerates had created for them, but it was familiar.

"You just planted Kafír Rosette," Kayleigh said in awe. "But that acorn… wasn't it from Kafír?"

Lincoln smiled, then said, "Tell it where you'd like to go."

Without hesitation, Kayleigh spoke.

"Take us back to *our* Mona."

The false liquid-fabric of the portal changed, rotating now in a slower, more complex ballet of hidden meaning.

"Let's go home," Kayleigh whispered.

They did not have to journey back through the woods of Burnam Tau'roh to reach the Oak Hotel. The dual Pandiments returned them to the small room off the kitchen—the very place they'd first met Mona. They smelled fresh bread, baking clams and something spicy stewing.

"It feels like we've been gone for years," Kayleigh said, sitting slowly down on a stool.

There was a sound from the archway that led into the kitchen. Looking up, they discovered a familiar woman watching them. Walking in, Mona gently embraced first Kayleigh, then Lincoln. Without speaking, she left the room and reappeared with a shallow, brown jar. Sitting, Mona scooped out a dab of strange, green paste and began to massage it into Kayleigh's wounded hands.

Kayleigh gasped, but after a brief, intense moment of heat, her hands grew numb. The pain was gloriously gone. She watched wide-eyed as Mona continued to work the salve into her skin. When Mona finished with Lincoln's hands, Kayleigh looked down at her own and saw that the rock-hard calluses and torn blisters were gone. Her hands were pinkish and new.

"We'll fix up the rest of you two a bit later," Mona said, setting the jar aside. She turned and looked straight at

Kayleigh. "Before we talk about anything else, I think it's time you finally met your Grandmother."

Mynah Corci's palm reading came back to her and she stared back at Mona.

"I'll go and tell her you're here. Just give me a minute, then walk down the main hall. She's in the last room on the right. I'm so sorry I've kept her hidden for so long…"

With a decidedly guilty look on her face, Mona left the room.

"Mona's acting strange," Lincoln said, gently moving his fingers and waiting for the pins-and-needles rush to subside.

"Not strange," Kayleigh said, rising from her seat. "Nervous."

"Nervous? Why?"

Kayleigh shook her head slowly from side to side and took a few steps toward the kitchen. "I'll show you. Come on."

Kayleigh led them from the kitchen out into the hallway. Turning right, they moved toward the pale light of a distant, open door. It was through this doorway that they first entered the Oak Hotel.

Lincoln wanted to ask what Kayleigh meant by nervous, but he couldn't get over how much better he felt now that his hands were healed.

They reached the end of the hall and stopped. A fresh breeze (redolent of sea-salt and pine) blew past the open door. Kayleigh turned to Lincoln and there were fresh tears welling in her eyes.

"You carried me," she said. "You carried me from Te'hæra Thorn, through the portal and back to Mount Aikona. You carried me from the Mountain all the way through the woods to Kafír's meadow. You made sure I was okay. You protected me."

She leaned forward and gently kissed him on the lips.

"When we go into that room, Lincoln, things might change. Or maybe they won't. I don't know. Our lives are so crazy. We never know what's going to happen and just get caught up in everything. But you know what? We're still Kayleigh Lambert and Lincoln Torres, right? We're still you and me. We're older, but we're still young—"

We were never children, Lincoln thought sadly, then reached out and put his hands gently on her shoulders.

" and I've always known how I felt about you. But now it's just too big a feeling to keep it all inside and wait, you know?"

Lincoln felt as if he were floating. With the pain gone, looking into Kayleigh's face was more of a dream than reality.

"I carried you... because I love you," he said.

Through a face clouded by dirt, grime and fatigue, Kayleigh smiled. He had never seen anything more beautiful in his life.

"You should probably open that door," Lincoln said.

"Only if you'll go in with me," she said.

And so, together, they entered.

The room was not illuminated by the powder blue haze of *foreverlights*, but instead by a large window on the north-facing wall. The remaining wall space was taken up completely by tightly packed shelves of books. At the far end of the room, a woman sat before a long, wooden desk. Before her were stacks of leather-bound volumes. Some were the same books they'd seen in the secret room off of Mona's kitchen in the past. One of them was open to a blank page. The woman turned to them and stood.

"Hello, Grandmother," Kayleigh said, holding onto Lincoln's left arm with both hands.

"Hello," replied Mona Tarok.

To be continued in…

The Lost

Boardwalk

The Chronicles of

Burnam Tau'roh

Book Four

Pronunciation Guide

Burnam Tau'roh – bur-NAHM TAH-row

de'Na – day-NAH

Kafír Rosette – ka-FEAR roh-SET

Te'hæra Thorn – tuh-HAY-rah THORN

Ka Tolerates – KAH toe-leh-RAH-tays

Kana Hove – kah-nah HOVE

de'Malange – day muh-LAHNJ

Mona Tarok – mow-nuh TAIR-ahk

Kell-Korai – kell kor-EYE

Shora Cessyu – shor-ah say-SOO

ghesthi'voult – GUESS-thee voo

sáwol – SAH-wall

Cast of Characters

Kayleigh Lambert – A twelve year-old girl from Autumn Harbor. She is on a quest to discover the secrets of her Grandmother's past and the mysterious de'Malange oak trees.

Lincoln Torres – A twelve year-old boy from Autumn Harbor. He is Kayleigh's best friend and companion on their quest.

Laura Corwin – Kayleigh's Grandmother.

Mona Tarok – The cook and keeper of the Oak Hotel and the Trokamano Orchard.

Rylyn – A mysterious young girl who helps Mona Tarok in the Trokamano Orchard.

Truman Stitch – The corrupt Mayor of Burnam Tau'roh. He has been infected with the dark energy of Ka Tolerates.

BTEL #3 – A locomotive train that runs on the Burnam Tau'roh Eastern Line.

Kafir Rosette – A mysterious, sentient tree hidden deep in the woods of Burnam Tau'roh.

Emil Corwin – Kayleigh's Grandfather.

Ka Tolerates – An evil tree that inhabited the Valley of the Oaks on Te'hæra Thorn.

Nova Reckór – The Mayor of Burnam Tau'roh before Truman Stitch takes the seat. She befriends Kayleigh and Lincoln.

Mynah, Hymna and Ahnmy Corci – The reclusive, blind triplets who have to ability to read futures by reading a person's hand.

Ben and Joseph Tompkins – Father and son team who tend the Tompkins Apiary. Both befriend Kayleigh and Lincoln.

Pearle Kho – Denizen of Kana Hove who enlightens Kayleigh and Lincoln and aids in their quest.

Walter Klimczak is the author of *Falling in the Garden* and *This Place Only*, the first two books in the TimeFront series. He lives in Atlanta, Georgia with his wife and three children.

.